Pajr of Normal What?

Also by Southern Indiana Writers' Group

The Indian Creek Anthology Series:

Indian Creek Anthology

Ghost Writers

Christmas Bizarre

Dragon: Our Tales

Grounds for Suspicion

2000 Tales

Way Out West

Unbridled Lust

There's Something Under the Bedtime Stories

Novel Ingredients

Write of Passage

Off the Rack

Beastly Tales

It's Always Something

Most Wanted

Future Perfect: Tense in Space

Holiday Bizarre

Pair of Normal What?

The Worst Book in the Universe

XX: SIW Goes Platinum

Herding Cats and Other Alien Creatures

Also by SIW:

Ghosts: On the Square ... And Elsewhere

Visit the Authors at:

southernindianawriters.com

Pair of Normal What?

The Southern Indiana Writers' Group

SIW

Pair of Normal What?
Volume 18 of the Indian Creek Anthology Series

Copyright © 2013 Southern Indiana Writers

Each selection herein © 2013 by the author or artist

Published by Southern Indiana Writers, 2200 Reno Ave., New Albany, IN, 47150
Book designed by T. Lee Harris

ISSN 1085-357X
ISBN 978-0-9882664-1-4

Cover Art and design by T. Lee Harris

Pair of Normal What?

Contents

The Game

by Bonnie Abraham

Credit where credit is due: I could never have come up with the chess moves recorded in this story. They are from an actual game played in London in 1838 between Evans (white) and MacDonnell (black) as recorded in The Fireside Book of Chess, edited by Irving Chernev and Fred Reinfeld. I chose this particular game just because I like the arrangement of the pieces. So, pull out your chess board and follow along — if you dare.

First, you have to understand that I am not given to believing in magic and hoodoo and spirits — all that paranormal stuff. I mean really — give me a break. That said, I have to admit, last night was — well — strange, okay?

These two guys come into the cafe and sit at the corner table. They look like average Joes, nothing strange. They order coffee and pie — one lemon and one apple. I put napkins and forks down and go for their orders.

As I walk away, the dude with the beard pulls a cloth out of his coat pocket and spreads it on the table. I see that the cloth is white and black checked — big checks, about an inch and a half. The other guy, the one with the glasses, pulls a couple of bags out of his pockets. He hands one of the bags to the beard and then dumps his onto the cloth. Chess pieces.

I'm watching all this as I bring their coffee and dish up their pies. When I set the pies on the table I see that Beard has white and Glasses has black. I don't know much about chess — just how the pieces move and that each square on the board has a designation, so that moves can be logged. That part isn't hard. (You just have to remember to always count from the white side bottom to top and letter left to right. It only gets confusing when you're trying to reconstruct a game and you're looking at the board from black's side.) Anyway, I ask if I can watch the game.

They look at each other — kinda weird-like, and Glasses says, "If you want."

The first few moves are quick and, to me at least, meaningless. Pawn to e4, pawn to e5; then knight to f3, knight to c6; bishop to c4 and bishop to c5. White — that would be Beard — castles. Glasses doesn't castle; he smirks and moves pawn to d6. As though by agreement, they slide the chess cloth aside and tackle their pie. Outside, it begins to rain.

A young couple comes in, dripping and laughing. They take the table in the corner opposite the two playing chess. I grab my order book and go to see what they want. When I return, Glasses has finished his pie and Beard has moved his to one side. The chess game is back in the center of the table. I clear away the empty plate and refill the coffee. I see that Beard has moved a pawn to b4. Glasses picks up his bishop and slides the pawn aside, picks it up and deposits it on the table.

There is a loud crash of thunder and the lights flicker. Glasses grins. Beard carefully picks up the vanquished pawn, slides it into his bag, then moves pawn to c3. Glasses moves his bishop to a5. Pawn to d4, bishop to g4. Then they bring the queens out. Beard sends his to b3 and Glasses quickly moves to d7. At least the black queen ends up there; I don't see Glasses make the move. I thought I was watching but—

2

I glance over at the couple across the room. They're holding hands and feeding each other pie. They don't look like they need my help. I look back at the chess game and Beard's knight is now on g5 and Glasses' knight is at d8. It appears to me that Glasses is in retreat, but what do I know about strategy?

This time I don't look away and, I swear, the pieces move by themselves: the d4 pawn captures the pawn at e5 and the d6 pawn captures the white pawn e5. The lights dim again as thunder shakes the big window in front. An ambulance roars past, siren blaring. When I look back at the table, the captured pawns are gone — in their respective bags, I assume.

The other white bishop moves by itself to a3 and the black knight jumps to h6. Beard has both his hands wrapped around his coffee mug and is looking out the window. Glasses drums his fingers on the table, waiting for the next move.

As the white pawn on f2 moves to f3, Beard takes a leisurely bite of pie. Glasses looks up at Beard, who seems to be getting larger, and the black bishop moves to b6, attacking the white king.

The white king moves to h1 and Glasses snorts. His bishop moves to h5.

The white rook moves to d1, attacking the black queen; the black queen moves to c8, leaving the black knight on d8 exposed to the rook.

The white rook flies across the board and pushes off the knight. A fire truck pulls up in front of the window, lights flashing, sirens blaring. Glasses looks out and frowns but I'm watching the board now. I see the black knight burst into flame then disappear. As the black queen knocks the rook off the board, Beard reaches out and gently returns it to his bag. A bolt of lightning hits the building across the street, where a little storefront church is meeting, but the fire truck is already there, the firemen running into the building.

The white knight at g5 jumps to f7 and, as it lands, the pawn that occupied that square vanishes in a burst of light.

Glasses is growling and his eyes — you aren't gonna believe this, but it's true — his eyes turn red! His queen moves to h4, out of the reach of the knight. The white queen moves to b5, attacking the king. Glasses is smoking — and I'm not talking cigarettes.

The c7 pawn moves up to c6, blocking the white queen's attack, but the white queen moves to e5. The pawn that was on the square — you guessed it — another burst of light. The black king is under attack again. Beard, who by now looms like a giant over the table, takes another bite of his pie. He savors that bite as though it were the most important thing in the world. Glasses is not just smoking, flames are coming from his head!

The couple at the other table have finally picked up on something going on. The guy pulls out his wallet, slaps a twenty on the table and they almost run out the door. I'm thinking seriously about following them.

The black king scampers to temporary safety on d7, but even I know he's done for. The white queen moves to the adjacent e6, and the black king can't do a thing about it because she's protected by her bishop at c4. He ducks between his men at c7. I'm thinking, "You can run but you can't hide." The bishop at a3 moves to d6. Glasses is engulfed in flames and vanishes.

Outside, the rain stops. Beard, who is now back to normal size, carefully picks up the pieces, returning them to their bags. He folds up the cloth and puts it in his pocket, places a gold coin on the table, smiles at me, and — vanishes.

"Game over," I say to myself. I turn out the lights and lock up without cleaning. It will all be there tomorrow.

Rusalka

by Marian Allen

I take up my pen, if not with tranquility, at least with composure — surprising, perhaps, in light of the past night's events, if surprise were not by now beyond me.

Perhaps you will discount this as fictional. I would not blame you. I would envy your unbelief, the complacency which is so much more comfortable than the unnatural calm now left to me.

An opalescent moon shone like a precious stone on deep blue velvet. So bright it was, that the stars, which ordinarily sparked across the seaside country sky, paled. I have seen days that were dimmer than that night. Dear heaven, was it only last night?

So bright it was at midnight, when I dimmed the study lamp, I scorned my bedroom and went, instead, out into the dewy quietude, down to the inlet where my people came to catch fish for my dinner. The full moon's reflection floated upon its mirror surface, almost too lambent to look upon.

As I neared the water, the brilliant disk wavered, though there was no wind. The white circle rippled and rose, and resolved into a woman standing upon the surface. Was she dressed in white linen, which clung to her shape with the weight of its liquidity, or was she bare, wearing only inhumanly featureless flesh?

I could not say, but she was suddenly at the marshy edge, not illuminated by the moon above, but luminescent in herself. She held out her arms to me. She smiled, her lips red as coral.

"Who are you?" I thought, or perhaps I whispered it, for she smiled more broadly, showing teeth like pearls.

"Rusalka," she whispered back, or perhaps she only thought it, for I did not see her mouth form the word, and yet I heard it.

I stepped into the mud, into the water, into her arms, and she drew me close. The chill damp crept up my body as we glided out and down, until the sea burned my eyes and I lost sight of her empty gaze.

With that, I came to myself. I gasped and thrashed, raising my mouth above the surface long enough to fill my lungs with precious air before my succubus, with infernal strength, pulled me back into her domain, down, down to the very floor of the inlet.

There, I saw unspeakable things: the corpses of men — yes, and of children — lured to deaths by this creature's mesmerizing beauty. And, as I looked upon the hideous remains, I saw salvation. It was a blade: a fisherman's knife, still sheathed at a dead man's side.

I snatched it, drew it, held it before the phantom's face, pommel upwards, thrusting the shape of the Cross between damnation and myself.

Rusalka shoved herself away, the force sending me backward and upward. I broke the surface again, bellowing for air, weeping and praying as I flailed the eternal distance back to land.

I reached the fen that bordered the inlet and struggled toward solid ground. A cold hand clutched my shoulder and spun me around.

Again I raised my makeshift Cross and again the thing shrank back. Then the blood froze within my veins, for the monster lifted her head and laughed.

Laughter, I call it, for want of a better word, but no earthly laughter ever came so shrill and savage. The very beating of my heart slowed; my lungs refused to breathe, and I grew faint.

To save my life — to save my soul — I took a different grip upon my weapon. With the words, "Our Father, who art in heaven," on my lips, I spent my final strength in an arcing blow, slicing the shining throat with tempered steel.

Without a sound, she vanished. I dropped my weapon and collapsed.

And so I lay, alone and senseless, until my people, missing me in the morning, found me and carried me to my bed.

I told them I slipped and fell, having taken a foolish moonlight stroll. How could I tell them the truth? They would have thought me mad. Indeed, my only hope for sanity is that I, myself, may come to believe the events of the night just past only happened in a dreadful dream.

To that purpose, I have penned this account and, when I have written THE END, will consign it to the flames of my bedroom fire.

THE END

Birds Must Wonder

(when they smack into windows)
by J. Baumgartle

about planes of existence.
The air clearly freezes
mid-flight at odd times.
Indigo bunting, yellow finch
and scarlet tanager speculate
from a recovered perch.
What are those
like-feathered creatures,
beautiful, intense,
that hurl themselves
toward us, disappear
upon impact?
Are they caught
in their world,
or we in ours?
Must it always hurt?

Raven's Blood

by Ginny Fleming

The cloudy night sky swirled darkly beneath her wings as she made her descent, dropping out of the remains of a summer-warmed layer of air and flying swiftly over the ocean's dark surface. Her shiny black wing-feathers caught the moon's silver sparkle as it peeked through the clouds with a voyeuristic glee. She thrilled to the feel of the wind in her feathers and the sea mist in her tiny lungs.

Pushing herself, she swooped through the mist-cooled sky.

Slowing her speed, her expert wings took her to a tall tower's open window. Now safe in the palace, she hovered above the slight body of a sleeping girl. A moonbeam's fairy-light fell across the small bed softly illuminating the girl's jet-black hair.

The avian touched down upon the slumbering girl's chest and called softly in her bird-voice and melded into the peaceful child.

Her black beady eyes gazed at the sleeping face before her. Sneaking in through the tall window, a quick silver moonbeam danced over the girl's own jet-black hair. The moon's fairy-light likewise sparkled over the black-winged avian as it called softly, melding into the peaceful child.

The girl awoke, trembling in her small bed, a cold sweat beading her brow. "Wha . . . what?" Gazing about the room, she shivered, whispering aloud to the room. "Did I return too late? By Etherial's Locks, he must not know of this."

She hugged herself in the chill of the pre-dawn hour and hurried to dress by the light of the morning moon. The girl knew the palace would be stirring soon, and she wanted to be prepared for the moment that — without the courtesy of a simple knock — Ahzrrann turned the key in the locked and guarded entry. She knew he'd burst through the door as he did every morning, just as she knew the evil man did so hoping in his black heart to catch her unawares and naked in her embarrassment. she also knew, even though her body still bore more the signs of childhood than hints of the woman she was fast becoming, Ahzrrann enjoyed his tormenting pre-dawn tirades simply for the pleasure of her discomfort.

Everytime the door flew open, the guard posted outside the door never failed to snicker in anticipation of a brief voyeuristic glance of her innocent body. If for nothing else but his lustful laughter, The girl felt she could gladly kill the traitorous sentry — who'd once been her father's most trusted guard.

This morning, the girl heard the footsteps climbing the winding tower room stairs just as she'd finished adjusting the belt around her simple summer frock. The guard's greeting sounded and she draped her father's gift of a tiny heart-shaped gold locket around her neck. She would not be caught unawares today.

Ahzrrann turned the key in the lock and pushed the tower door open. "Ahhh, Little Raven. . . ." He sneered and her heart clutched at the sound of his unknowingly intuitive choice of faux-endearment. "I see you're already up with the morning birds. First to snare the worm today? Good. I'm sure breakfast will be to your liking."

The tall man wore her father's stolen highborn robes and he laughed wickedly as an old woman sat a platter and tankard on the table. Jherri recognized the weary servant as her dead brother Chandel's childhood governess. Head down submissively, the old woman's eyes met Jherri's and sent a silent message of apology to the girl.

The girl returned the soundless glance: No need to sorrow, Old Maggie. Both of us are coping as best we can.

The dirty plate bore one crusty slice of dried brown bread and a pale hunk of moldy cheese. A greasy tankard held a draft of bitter and stale ale to wash the scrapes down. First meal had been such since Ahzrrann slaughtered her brothers and wrested the kingdom from her father's dying hands.

"Thank you, Ahzrrann." Jherri smiled at the oily man standing before her making a mockery of her father's station in life. "Thank you for the beautiful first meal you have prepared for me."

The old woman flashed the barest of smiles at the girl before hurrying from the room.

Ahzrrann scowled. "Has sleep changed your mind, then, Little Raven? Shall we dispense with these useless games? Are you prepared to tell me where your father's priceless treasure is hidden, or are you prepared to spend yet another week in this dismal room with the window set high above your head? You do miss sight of your precious ocean, do you not?"

"I still have senses remaining to me, Ahzrrann," Jherri smiled again, forcing herself to nibble the old bread. "I can hear the breaking waves, as well as smell and taste the sea on the wind. On some nights, if I close my eyes, I swear I can even see the rolling waters breaking upon the dark shore —"

"Do you think I'll wait forever, girl?" he interrupted her. Gone was the faux-endearment, replaced with his anger. "Your body can be broken, just as the bones of the males of your family. With one tiny exception. First, you'll be given to Fedden, as payment for his diligent watch outside your door. I've heard he's a very generous man. He shares his playthings with the other guards—"

"Do you think," Jherri likewise interrupted the angry man using a tone so like his own in mockery, "your pitiful threats will wear me down? What more can you do to me? You gained my father's favor, rose to undermine his power. You betrayed his trust, killed him and my beloved brothers, locked me away — and you think to do more? Oh, Ahzrrann. Such a foolish man. You have won a hollow victory and still you can not see it. I am beaten."

"You'll tell me where the treasure is hidden?"

"Would that I could, Oh Mighty Ahzrrann, Muderer of Children. Other than the gold and jewels you took from my father's bloody corpse, I fear there is no more." She again nibbled on the barely edible bread crust. "This was not a wealthy kingdom. My father was not a hoarder of riches. He always swore the wealth of a kingdom was in the joy of its people, not in the pockets of its king."

"You little liar."

"Believe what you will, Ahzrrann." Jherri sighed and took a sip of the bitter ale. "I've been told it is as easy to die for no treasure as to die for great piles of gold. I'll be dead just the same and for just as long. Don't you agree?"

"Such brave words from one so small." Ahzrrann regained his composure and his oily sneer. "The fire in you is not easily extinguished. Perhaps I should have employed my first plan instead. Asking for your hand in marriage. In his fawning over you, even your father would have preferred the chief adviser to the court jester for a son-in-law."

"Thomas is a minstrel — not a court jester!" She cried out with more emphasis than intended. She'd hoped to maintain an aloofness of quiet dignity around this man whom she hated with a passion. Many times in the past, her father had counseled: "*Always remember, my daughter. Dignity is one's only true possession. It can't be stolen, Little Raven,*" he'd said, "*the owner is the only one who can give one's dignity away.*"

"Ahhh. . . . So you do have a weakness. Perhaps I shall have to search out the jester. Perhaps he has knowledge of the hidden treasure. Or perhaps," the man taunted, "my gentle persuasion of him shall jog your memory." His corruption clung to his presence like a live-thing, born in unholy nativity, spawned from the very loins of Baal.

"You are evil, Ahzrrann. Even your mother cursed your name as she birthed you."

"You flatter me, Little Raven," Ahzrrann chuckled, running his hand down the length of Jherri's black tresses.

She forced herself to remain ridged and did not flinch to his touch, nor to his mocking use of the pet name favored by her father.

Ahzrrann let his cold hand linger on her shoulder, kneading her soft skin with a slimy familiarity. "We shall see how your bravery fills your stomach when the food is not placed before you."

He stroked her cheek and Jherri shuddered in spite of her self-restraint. How she hated him! Her fondest wish was a dagger to plunge into his black heart and the chance to twist it before he died. The image of Ahzrrann writhing in the throes of a painful death near brought a smile to her lips, though, she quelled the fantasy until a time of solitude.

"Are you not going to fall at my knees and beg me continue these fine meals, Princess?" He bent to her ear, breathed his lustful hot breath across her face and whispered, "Beg me?"

"I would not beg for such slop, Ahzrrann. I'd rather whither to bone than give you the pleasure."

"So be it," he chuckled again. "I'll leave you to your thoughts and sea-mist. I believe a week or two of my absence will make your heart grow fonder — or at least your stomach will cry welcome to my return."

He turned and made for the door, halted and reversed himself, taking the platter and tankard from the table. "We must not leave a mess. Is it not so, Little Raven?" Sharing a laugh with Fedden, the guard, Ahzrrann locked the door, sealing Jherri into the tiny room.

That evening, before true darkness fell over the Kingdom, she flew from the tower's window. Her strong wings silently beat the thin air, carrying her over the ocean. She glided low along the shoreline, plucking small fish from the sea-foam with her sharp talons, making a ballet of the catch.

Swoop, sight, snare and pull free from the salty water. Soon her tiny bird-belly was full and she returned to perch on the tower window's ledge and she gazed down at the sleeping child she'd left in the bed.

Her evenings were spent feeding and her nights were spent gliding over the waters and grounds around the castle, searching for signs of Thomas, her minstrel. She had to find him before Ahzrrann did — but how would he know her when she found him?

###

The next night, before she lay down in the bed, Jherri took the locket from her neck and closed the clasp tighter. Making the chain much shorter, she placed it on the bare table. As she felt sleep overtake her, the girl sniffed the air for her beloved sea-mist and whispered dreamily, "Glide over the water. . . ."

Within moments the bird appeared and hopped to the table. Cocking her bird head to the side, she spied the locket she'd modified moments before and dipped her beak, scooping the chain up over her shiny black head. The locket now hung from her feathered neck and rested against her tiny breastbone. She took wing and flew out the window for her nightly feeding.

Her search for Thomas proved fruitless. She cried her frustrations and fears to the heavens in her bird voice, sounding like just another ocean bird swooping over the dark sandy shore. Surely, if she could not find Thomas, he must be in hiding and if he were safe from her sharp avian eyes, he would be safe from Ahzrrann as well.

Jherri spent the next two weeks and two days locked in the solitude of the tower, feeding in the bounty of her beloved ocean. When Ahzrrann finally turned the key in the lock, throwing the door wide, she sat up in the bed — already dressed in her summer frock — and she smiled sleepily at him. "So nice to see you, Ahzrrann."

"I'll wager your hunger greets me most of all, Little Raven." He stepped across the floor and stood at her bedside, towering over her. "Tell me of your father's precious treasure and I will see the finest meats and best ales brought to your parched lips — " He looked down at the girl sitting upright in the bed. "Why, I swear by the Eyes of Shadeen! Your cheeks have color and your bones are not wasted — what kind of witchery is this?"

"No witchery, Ahzrrann." She smiled and stood from the bed. "The spirits of my dear father and beloved brothers sustain me. They reach out from the grave and mock you, Oh Murderer of Innocents."

"Foolish girl!" Ahzrrann sputtered, though he glanced around the room as if he could not help but search out vengeful spirits.

She gazed up into his dark eyes, seeing a flash of doubt and fear — and Jherri smiled to herself. Perhaps this isn't a dagger, but I'll twist it just the same! "My father's spirit visits me nightly, Ahzrrann," she lied, the words leaving her lips easily. "He will not rest until your vile heart ceases its beating and your evilness is wiped from this fair land, for his soul cries vengeance!"

She forced herself to look the hated man directly in the eyes. "Have you heard my father's death-vows in your dreams? Have you heard the cries of my brothers? Know you, my youngest brother was but a child?"

Ahzrrann averted his eyes as Jherri continued her tirade. She stepped in front of the tall man, commanding his attention, compelling him to gaze down into her brown eyes. Her voice was almost a whisper, made more sharp by the remembrance of witnessing her beloved brother's screams.

She clutched Ahzrrann's arm — though to touch him sickened her heart — and she hissed: "His toys were put aside mere seasons when he tasted the bite of your sword. Have you heard his innocent tears? Have you heard Chandal weeping in your dreams?"

"Lies!!" Ahzrrann hissed, color rising to his face. "Lies!! Witch-Spawn of a dead king! I shall not listen to the lies of a witch! Perhaps by the light of the next full moon your lips will not be so ready to spew fantasies when they have not tasted water nor meat. Let your martyred father feed you a few more weeks, Witch! When next I return, it shall be to gaze at your wasted corpse."

So saying, Ahzrrann stalked from the room, slamming the door behind him. Jherri smiled. The oily man had made no mention of Thomas; surely that meant he'd not found the minstrel. She sat back on the bed, closed her eyes and pictured the ocean swirling outside her window.

She called to mind the tiny boat Thomas had built with his own hands to take her sailing over the water. He'd named it "Little Raven", the name taken from the King's pet name for his favorite daughter.

The girl laughed fondly of the memory, for after all, that day she'd snuck out of the castle to go sailing. On that joyous morning, Thomas sent her into muffled gales of laughter by pretending they were escaping a villain close on their heels. How ironic. How she wished she could now run from Ahzrrann. She brought her thoughts back to her sweet minstrel and his wonderful sailboat.

That beautiful day, the day Thomas and Jherri sailed in the warm sunshine, she'd felt certain he was ready to ask for her hand. He spoke of their future together, far away, in a village by the sea. Thomas vowed they'd make their living fishing and selling sea-treasures, shells and pearls, weaving a fantastic fantasy while their tiny craft skated over the calm water.

###

Now, locked in her tower prison, Jherri told herself she wasn't mistaken — she hadn't dreamed it; Thomas had been prepared to ask her father — his king — for her hand. His common blood be damned. But, Ahzrrann, in his evil, made certain the question would never be asked.

Before Jherri's dark-haired minstrel of the blue eyes could speak and declare his love, her father lay in a cold grave, alongside her brave brothers and many in the Kingdom who were loyal unto death. And unable to find her in the confusion, Thomas had fled in the "Little Raven", the very night of the slaughter.

Her daydreams and memories carried her through the day until the shadows creeping through the tall window testified to the coming evening. Jherri fell into an easy slumber, the bird appeared, the locket hanging from its neck, and it flew out the tower window.

She fed well that night and after many joyous swoops over her beloved ocean, the black bird perched outside the tower window on a pepper tree branch. She sat reveling in the night sounds, the crickets, the tree frogs, the songs of the flying lizards, the breaking of the waves upon the shore, when suddenly she heard the cry of a strange bird and looked down from her tree perch into the face of her beloved.

Thomas stood beneath the pepper tree looking up at the tower window, making their secret sounds. They'd practiced these bird calls together, Thomas telling her the trills and whistles were their code and theirs alone. He'd come for her, as she knew he would.

She swooped down to him, a happy cry leaving her beak, but the minstrel looked up to see a black falcon-sized bird diving at his head and he swatted her away.

20

Jherri was dismayed. She again perched on the branch over Thomas' head and peered down at him with ebony eyes. How could she let him know her true identity? The voice Thomas would recognize was locked in the tower room in the body of a sleeping girl. If he were to know her, she would have to sing the strange bird calls.

Her first attempts sounded harsh and gull-like even to her bird ears and Thomas merely continued brushing her away, though she remained safely out of his reach. Finally, after several attempts, she heard the sounds of the strange bird she'd found so simple to copy with her human lips leave the beak she now wore. Again she trilled the code.

"What's this, now?" Thomas whispered. "Are you a mocking bird, Little Warrior? Do you copy my song merely to flatter me?"

Jherri's tiny heart beat with hope as she again trilled the code of the strange bird.

"My, but you're a fast learner," Thomas whispered and smiled up into the tree. "My Lady Jherri failed to learn it so quickly."

Yet again, Jherri trilled the code, this time swooping from the tree to land upon Thomas' shoulder.

"Ahhh, a friendly warrior," Thomas murmured, lifting his hand to stroke the bird's feathered head. "Someone has trained you well...." He touched the chain draped around the bird's neck, and looked to the window overhead.

"Jherri's locket," he whispered. "I'd know it anywhere. Are you my Lady's bird? Dispatched from her hand to fly from my Love's locked room to find me? Old Maggie sent word, for want of the King's most precious treasure, Ahzrrann sealed Jherri away to die. Have you come to lead me to my Lady, Little Warrior?"

Jherri cocked her bird head to the side and looked into his eyes with one black beady orb.

"I sense an intelligence about you," Thomas murmured still stroking her black feathered head. "Can you tell me, little bird, how my Jherri fares?"

Jherri gazed into her minstel's blue eyes and loosed a mournful cry from her feathered throat.

"You learned the code so easily," Thomas mused. "Perhaps I can teach you another trick. Shall we say a whistle for yes and a peep for no?"

Jherri brightened. Her Thomas was indeed quick of mind. She whistled once, then whistled again, flapping her wings in excitement.

"Fine. . . ." Thomas placed his hand beneath Jherri's claws and removed her from his shoulder to sit upon his wrist. "Let us begin, Little Warrior. Are you sent from my Lady's prison cell?"

She whistled low and waited for the next question. The night brought many questions, many whistles, many peeps. By the time the sun began to brighten the horizon, Thomas learned with incredulity the girl who owned his heart now perched upon his wrist in the body of a black bird bearing a fine gold locket draped around her neck.

"Jherri, my dear one," he whispered as the first of the morning sunbeams brightened the outer tower wall, "I can not gain your freedom alone. Ahzrrann is much too powerful for a man who earns his living by song. I shall have to take you to the wise man of the ocean. Come. We shall set sail for his island in my boat."

The man carried the bird to the boat he'd earlier pulled up to the sandy shore. Thomas placed Jherri inside the small craft and shoved it off the beach, hopping in beside her as the bow caught the wave. They silently washed out to sea and the minstrel raised the tiny sail to catch the wind. The man and bird would be on the island seeking the wise man's council before the noon sun was high in the cloudless sky.

###

As Thomas and his winged lady sailed away from the castle, Ahzrrann again turned the key in the lock, shoving the door open. This time he found the girl still asleep, her breathing slow and easy.

"Ahhh, Little Raven. . . ." he began, hoping to wake her in a moment of fright. She didn't stir. He reached out his hand, tracing the curve of her cheek, and still Jherri failed to stir.

"Playing at the habits of the possum, my young one? Perhaps, I have ways to gain your attention." Again, he reached his hand out, but this time instead of stroking her cheek, he roughly tweaked the girl's budding nipple through her thin nightdress. Still . . . she failed to stir.

"By Dakkar's Twin Stones — I have tired of such folly!" Drawing his dagger, he roared out his frustration. "Hunger doesn't phase you, pain or lust doesn't rouse you. Perhaps my dagger's thrust will show you the delights awaiting as death claims you! First in your heart, Witch! Then, before breath has left your body, you shall feel my stronger shaft deep within your core!"

He brought the dagger down swiftly. Falling upon Jherri's small body, he stabbed her just under her right breast, growling in rage as he did so, expecting, hoping, to hear her tortured screams of death ring in his ears. Still she didn't stir. He raised his head from her jet-black hair where he'd buried his face and expectantly looked down, hoping to witness the dying girl's last gasp of agony.

She wasn't there! Instead of a murdered princess, Ahzrrann found he lay atop a strange black bird, its wings spread wide in death, his dagger buried deep in its tiny breastbone.

Out on the water, the small sailboat glided silently toward the island. Thomas stared at the bow of the tiny boat, not quite believing his eyes. There before him sat his life's love, in her thin nightdress, sprawled across the small sea-craft's bench. Her hands grasped her gold locket, clutching it to her breast. Jherri's eyes were closed as if in pain.

"My love. . . ." Thomas began.

"Oh, Thomas!" Jherri opened her eyes and cried. She allowed her troubadour to take her into his arms. "Raven is dead — Ahzrrann has indeed claimed Father's most precious treasure. Father always swore his changeling daughter as his hidden prize, but no one save my father and my brothers knew of my birthright and talent. Ahzrrann, in his great stupidity and ignorance has destroyed me. I am but a shell of my former self. Half my soul is gone!"

"Nonsense, my Beloved." Thomas soothed her, kissing her forehead. "Take half of mine, then you shall be whole once more."

"You don't understand, sweet Thomas," Jherri moaned. "I shall never again be able to soar over the ocean. . . ."

"So, you'll have to sail over the blue water's surface just as the rest of us mere humans." He smiled and kissed her again. "Hold tight to me, Little Warrior and we shall glide over the gentle waves together — on the wings of love."

###

Jherri and her minstrel of the blue eyes continued their short journey, not only to seek council from the wise man, but to ask his blessing upon the union of a Princess who was once a bird and a man who made his coin from a song.

Rainy Days and Mondays
by Dirk Grffin

i carried death
in a fat
mustard-colored car
cruising through
thick rains.
He made me
play The Carpenters
on the 8-track because
he despised radio.

*Talkin' to myself
and feelin' old*

"Have some scotch,"
he slurred.
i said, "You're here;
the last thing i need
is scotch."

Headlights blurred
through the wet panes;
we argued about whether
i'd missed a turn.

*Hangin' around,
nothin' to do but frown*

It was then we
caught the train
shearing off the nose
of that boxy, ugly car.

i hated that car.

The best part is,
i won't have to hear
him bitch about his
ex-girl-friend
anymore.

Aesthete

by J. Baumgartle

The steam room felt *so* good. He'd been cold all day; even his workout hadn't made him actually sweat. He parked himself across from Ed, who steamed like the Ghost of Christmas Present.

"How's it going, Harold?" Ed murmured.

"Fine, fine," Harold answered, exhaling a pressurized breath.

"Give it a few minutes," Ed told him. "You won't have a care in the world."

At this point, Harold couldn't even lean back.

"Hey, aren't you the one with the new wife, the college education, the great job? — Relax!"

Harold attempted a laugh.

"Wish I had your problems." The older man closed his eyes and smiled.

"No you don't."

"Do, too," and at the continued silence added "Give me a hint here, what are we talking about?"

"My wife," Harold admitted.

"What? That cute little gal? It's only been a few weeks — give it time."

"I thought I had," Harold responded.

###

Maybe two months weren't enough of an engagement, he mused. When he met Marcy, she worked at the coffee house, and he liked coffee, liked her bringing it to him. She was cute and fun and easy to be with. They went out a couple of times, and then sort of made it into a routine. She was a pleasant, comfortable cap to his evenings while he was working so hard finishing school. How sweet life would be, he imagined, with a home of his own and her for a companion–a warm, peaceful retreat. . . .

Graduation had made him feel "set up," along with the position he managed to walk into — and Marcy, to complete the picture.

They'd bought a log house, in a "wooded" subdivision of log homes. There he'd begun his ideal life.

This is intolerable. Her splendid hide rippled as it was stroked, though there was little more to it now than the map of her excellent markings. Nera tightened her throat in a crimped growl no one could hear. Everything about this creature sickened her. Its voice pooled in the air, its touch was random, with no purpose. Why would it stroke the dead?

Nera was almost overwhelmed by the indignity of it all, her helplessness, her loss. The urge to attack heaved uselessly under the pink fingers' touch. She could almost feel the rough terrain of her own territory under her paws, the huge range she had established as her own, the winds that blew across it, the grasses she hid in, the water, cool on her tongue. Her last mating had given her twins, that were now left on their own, defenseless, hungry, taken away from her in an instant by that sharp bolt. How cruel to endure the fawning perpetrated upon this dreamless self by this smelly creature with no markings.

They took a quick honeymoon trip to Cancun, and then Harold was scheduled to go to Pittsburgh, for two weeks of

28

orientation. All he had time for was to unpack and pack again. His few possessions, along with Marcy's, lined one side of their bedroom. Their opened wedding presents, some still half-wrapped, filled much of the remaining space. Among the more notable of these was a genuine leopard-skin, complete with head and shiny teeth. Harold was appalled at having the skin of an endangered species on the floor. Marcy's Uncle Wes took going on safari seriously; so Marcy would have the job of writing a thank-you note for it, and for everything else that still had an identifying tag.

As to furnishing the house, Harold envisioned a rather understated Shaker style, with woven accents and natural light . . . like brush strokes in the background where a few comfy contemporary pieces would be at home. Web sites offered the basics. Accordingly, he gave Marcy his new platinum card, and promised her that it wasn't hard to order stuff. Just click on what you wanted, set a date for delivery, and have things carried into the garage. He'd help her move the big pieces when he returned.

Coming home was sort of a dizzying experience. Harold stood in the doorway, trying to take it all in. Everything was pink and purple. The entire interior was fluffy with faux Thomas Kinkaid. After a long moment, he worked up the nerve to step inside. The hardwood floor was now carpeted, (the leopard skin transferred to the bed) under a sofa and chairs with floral upholstery. Tiny little pastel lamps and effusive floral arrangements hid every flat surface, and plaques with saccharine little platitudes were tacked up everywhere, in the bathrooms and hallways, in the kitchen and laundry-room. He plopped himself down on a pillowy chair. A painting from one of those "starving artist" sales, hung over the couch, a florid study in mint green, yellow, pink and lavender.

Coming home from the office was like a lesson that had to be relearned every day.

###

No matter how much you wanted to accommodate someone and recognize them as a person with individual tastes and ideas and needs, Harold realized, it was a daunting task. Change would be slow to come, if it ever did, and much of it would be up to him. What surprised him, was that Marcy was trying as well. The distance they felt between them bent occasionally, shifted one direction and then the other. Marcy asked his advice, let him tell her about his day, kept coffee made. Her day, apparently, involved keeping up with the family, trying new recipes, and doing household chores.

He could have whatever he wanted from his wife at night, but was unwilling to commit to starting a family. This, Marcy seemed okay with, except for a certain wistfulness that she brought to bed with her. The tensions of the day, and weariness, let them get more nights of sleep than either really wanted. Quiet hung in the air around them, unasked questions, initiative moderated into guesswork.

Each of them lay there sleepless, wondering, wishing, until Marcy reached for the leopard skin, drew it to her chin, and turned away.

###

Nera, however, had no pity to spare. She was clutched awkwardly, restless as the two silent creatures that paced the border of one territory, dragging at each other's needs. Life did not forgive hesitation. —The male musk was driving her crazy. If the numbed female didn't know the meaning of scent, she did. All her leopard instincts surged into the hot body beneath her, ravaged salt of salt, blood of blood, leaving the patterned skin to slide to the floor unnoticed.

Demon Ozone

by Marian Allen

A little girl with ringlets blue
And eyes of deepest gold
Approached the noisesome space canteen
And shivered with the cold.

She pulled a rag of green lamé
About her shoulders thin.
She pushed aside the swinging door
And then the child went in.

What sights are these to greet the eyes
Of one of tender years!
What sounds are these, from ev'ry side,
To fall on tender ears!

The worthless of a hundred worlds
Were crowding 'round the taps
Or seated at the tables dim
With girls upon their laps.

So, in amongst the revelers,
The gold-eyed urchin came
Until she reached a drunken man
Intent upon a game.

His hair had faded to pastel,
His eyes were shot with black.
The infant raised her tiny hand
And touched him on the back.

"Oh, father, dear," the child then said,
In accents mild and sweet,
"Please come back home. Mamma is ill,
And nothing's there to eat."

His eyes filled with repentant tears,
He fell upon his knees.
"And would you have me back?" he cried.
His daughter answered, "Please."

Oh, keeper of the space canteen,
Dispensing potions wild,
Pray God for grace, and think upon
The little Spaceman's Child!

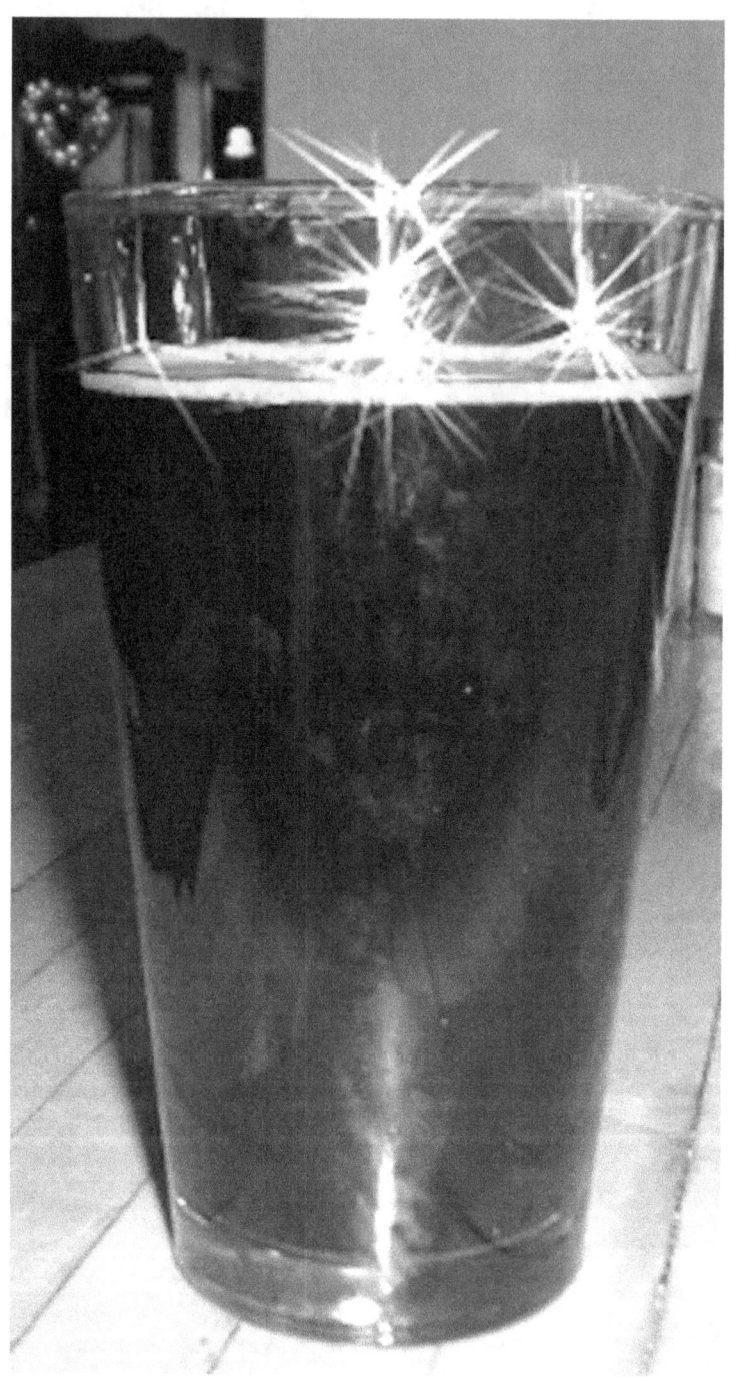

The Copse

by T. Lee Harris

The copse stood at the back of the park as it had for as long as anyone could remember. The rest of the park was manicured with careful plantings of smaller trees and border plants. The copse was wild and shaggy by comparison; the huge old oak at its center standing tall like a dark shepherd over graceful birches and unruly flocks of holly and brambles. In all the renovation the park had undergone, time and time again, the copse was spared the axe, and the bulldozers rumbled around, but never through.

That suited Maureen McKinney just fine. She slowed her determined walk as she entered the cool shade of the trees, enjoying the respite from the sun that beat down on the rest of the walking path. Lowering herself onto the metal mesh bench, she frowned at the walking stick in her hand. It was an ugly, utilitarian thing given to her by her surgeon. The aluminum shaft was sturdy, and did its job, but it had no class — no soul. Sighing, she leaned the cane against the armrest of the bench, but it slipped. She grabbed at it, missed and it hit the pavement with a metallic crash.

Suddenly the park bench was gone. Instead, she was in a wrecked car, trapped by twisted metal. Flashing lights glared through her closed eyelids painting red and blue flashes on her foggy mind. Hard rain hissed against the cracked windshield. She opened her mouth to scream, but was choked by the stench of spilled gasoline and her own blood. Just as suddenly, she was back on the bench with the scent of sun-warmed grass and blooming wildflowers drifting over her on the gentle breeze. It took another full minute to still her racing heart and a bit more to convince her hands to unclench the edge of the seat. She leaned back, breathing in the peaceful aromas and cursing the flashbacks that had tormented her since the terrifying night of twisted metal and broken glass that had taken her fiancé, shattered her body and changed her life.

"Well, that was just wonderful, Mo," she muttered. "You let the fear win another round. Good thing no one was here to see you fall apart. Again." Choking back tears, she snatched the cane off the path, sat back, closed her eyes and breathed in the scent of the wood and wildflowers. It seemed to heal her in some way, bringing a small amount of peace with each inhalation. Sitting like that, she could be anywhere and any time. She could be in a time and place where the accident hadn't happened. Where she was preparing to walk down the aisle with the love of her life instead of learning to walk all over again.

Longing washed over her and she lost herself in the wish until: "Mo! YOOOHOO! Mo!"

Wrenched back to the here and now, she opened her eyes to see her best friend, Shauna, jogging toward her across the grass.

Shauna laughed. "Where were you, Girl? I've been calling and calling."

Mo smiled. "I was a million miles away."

Shauna flopped down on the bench beside her. "This is a good place for it. Seems more peaceful here than any other spot." Turning to look over the back of the bench, she said, "Y'know, if this bench faced the other way, you'd think you were in a meadow instead of a park in the middle of the city."

Mo looked back, too, and nodded. "It's these trees. They've seen so much, it's all old hat to them." She regarded the spring-bright green leaves dancing against the huge, rough trunks for a bit, then turned to her friend, saying, "I'm surprised to see you. I didn't think you could make it today."

"I'm surprised to be here. The plumber actually came when he said he would. I'm damn glad of it, too. I hate spending my days off waiting around. So have you made a lap, yet?"

"I made three."

Shauna's eyes widened. "All right!"

"My best so far." Mo allowed herself some pride. "That's the whole purpose of coming here, isn't it? To strengthen my legs?"

"Looks like I need to catch up, then. If you want to wait here on the bench—"

"Not on your life!" she said with a huge grin. "I've rested on my as — I mean *laurels* long enough. I'm ready to go again." Mo levered herself off the bench and stood, nodding toward two cars disgorging kids by the play set. "We better hurry, too. The place is filling up. If we wait too long we'll be dodging toddlers all the way around."

"Toddlers I can deal with," Shauna said frowning in the other direction, "but we might have to dodge more deliberate obstacles. Like flying skateboards?"

Mo's heart fell. She followed her friend's gaze to where a tall, gangly teenage boy was talking to a group of other kids. He had numerous facial piercings and was dressed in deliberately wrecked clothes that bagged around his rail-thin frame. Still, he would have been a good-looking boy if not for the permanent scowl on his face. "Oh no. Jimmy McNeal. And it was such a good day."

"If he gets nasty, we'll just walk on and ignore him. Words are just forced air, Girl." Shauna paused, and shook her head. "It must be terrible to be that full of hate and anger. How could you live with yourself?"

Pajr of Noumal What?

"I wish I could be as charitable as you. I'd call him just plain mean. That skateboard he kicked at us last week could have done some serious damage."

"IF it had hit." Shauna's eyes crinkled in a smile. "Which it didn't, thanks to someone going all Daredevil with her cane and blocking it."

Mo sneered at the aluminum stick in her hand. "Ugly thing. Needs to be good for something other than helping me keep my balance."

"If that thing bugs you so much, why don't you get another? There are all sorts of pretty ones on the 'Net."

"No way! I've graduated from wheelchair, to walker, to this thing and I plan to ditch *this* thing as soon as I can. If I get a pretty one, I won't want to put it away."

Shauna stepped back onto the path. "Mo logic. You can't argue with it. Hey, if we're going to walk, we better get moving."

Mo knew something was wrong as soon as they turned the bend that took them near the basketball courts. A knot of upset and shrieking kids stood just to one side of the path. A few of the younger ones were crying. Over this, rose a braying laugh that both women recognized immediately. McNeal. This spelled trouble because McNeal never laughed unless it was at someone else's expense. The two women slowed and glanced at each other nervously.

"I feel like such a coward to let a kid like that make me want to walk the other way," Mo said.

Shauna opened her mouth to answer, but never got the chance.

The screams pierced again and McNeal shouted, "Ooooh! Cry now. Just watch what I do to the little furball next."

38

To Mo's horror, a small furry body was flung into the air. It looked like a very young cat, black and white, too dazed to escape.

One of the older girls shouted an obscenity and grabbed for the little animal, but McNeal snatched it out of the air just short of her hands. Laughing in her face, he shoved her down, threw the cat to the ground and raised his thick-soled boot over it.

Mo was moving before she realized it. Adrenaline propelled her, cane clutched like a weapon, she closed the distance as the boy's foot descended and threw herself into him. The impact knocked him sprawling several feet away to a smattering of cheers and laughter.

Snatching the dazed kitten up, she spat, "It really takes a big man to pick on a tiny animal." Before she knew what she was saying, she heard Shauna's words coming from her lips, "It must be terrible to be so full of hate and anger. How can you live with yourself?"

Jimmy McNeal picked himself up, angry eyes locked on Mo.

He reached for something in his pocket, but never completed the move as one of the other boys pointed and yelled, "SHIT! It's the cops!"

Mo swiveled with the boy's point. A police cruiser pulled up on the road that ran along the high embankment in back of the stand of ancient trees. Two officers, a man and a woman, stepped out as several residents of the houses that faced the park hurried toward them gesturing in Mo's direction. In an instant, Mo, Shauna and the girl McNeal had knocked down were alone. Just as abruptly, Mo's adrenaline rush vanished, leaving her rubber-legged and staggering. The injured cat in her arms mewed pitifully as Shauna rushed to her side and guided her to a bench.

"Wow! Just wow," Shauna said, running a hand through her close-cropped hair. "That was some sprint. Are you okay?"

Mo took a deep breath to steady herself. It didn't work. Her voice still shook as she answered, "It was pure adrenaline. It got the job done, but I'll pay for it later."

"Yes, Ma'am, you will. Been there, done that and they were all out of t-shirts," said a female voice off to her left. Glancing up, she saw the police officers walking briskly toward them. As they approached, the woman officer said, "Hi, folks, I'm Officer Wicks. This is my partner Officer Bishop." Jerking her thumb over her shoulder she added, "The folks who live back that way reported a disturbance brewing."

"They were right, but as soon as you guys arrived, everyone took off," Shauna said.

Officer Bishop quirked a half-smile. "They usually do. We'll need some statements, though, if you ladies would oblige."

The girl looked up from brushing herself off. "I'm not sure . . . I have to get home. . . ."

Officer Bishop's half-smile grew into a grin as he pulled a pen and note pad out of his pocket. "No problem. I'll interview you first." He led the reluctant girl to a bench a short distance away.

Wicks opened her own notebook and said to Shauna, "I'll start with you, Ma'am, and let your friend get her breath back."

As usual with something that happens quickly, the telling of it took longer than the event. Mo was glad the policewoman gave her time to rest before her turn came. The time spent sitting and holding the injured cat let the remaining adrenaline subside and her head clear. It also let her calm the trembling animal and give it a gentle inspection. When Officer Bishop and the girl returned to where she sat, she told the girl, "I think your cat will need to see a vet. Its front leg might be broken."

The girl shook her head. "It's not my cat. It's a stray that McNeal grabbed out of the alley, I just didn't want to see that creep hurt another animal." With that she hurried off without a backward look.

Officer Wicks watched the girl cross the park as she closed her notebook and tucked it back into her pocket. At length she said softly, "I agree with her, that kid's bad news. I dread the day he graduates from animals to people." She shook off the mood and turned back to Mo and Shauna. "Are you ladies going to be okay?"

"Yes, thanks," said Mo. "We just live up the block from here. We'll be fine."

The microwave dinged. Mo popped the door and removed a plate of fragrant cinnamon rolls. The cat, now named Domino and sporting a pink and white cast on one front leg, clunked across the kitchen's terra-cotta tiles following the aromas. He skidded to a stop in front of Mo and meowed pitifully.

Mo laughed and said, "Not yours, little guy. Your kitty crunchies are over there in your bowl." Placing the plate of pastries on the table between herself and Shauna, she told her friend, "I owe you big time for hauling me and Domino to the vet and the pet store."

Shauna set down her coffee mug and waved the thanks away. "Don't worry about it. You've done enough favors for me in the past. Besides, the little guy has pitiful down pat. How could I not do it? I'm glad you decided to adopt him, or I might have had to. That would have been rough on him with my work schedule."

The little cat whacked a tinkle ball and chased after it, seemingly unencumbered by the cast. Mo smiled. "My therapist has been after me to get a pet for months now. He said taking care of someone else would get my mind off of my own troubles. He says it isn't good for me to be alone so much."

Domino pranced up and tried to climb into Mo's lap, but the cast wouldn't let him. She lifted him up and said, "Don't worry, Little Bit, you'll get used to that cast. I know whereof I speak."

The cat squeaked to get down, so she set him carefully back onto the floor. As soon as his feet touched the tiles, he was off after the ball again.

Shauna sipped coffee and frowned over the rim of her cup. "It was wild hearing my own words coming out of your mouth. They seemed to hit that kid like a fist, too. Hope you didn't just paint a target on yourself."

"Don't you mean a *bigger* one? I already had one," Mo said breaking apart a roll, releasing cinnamon-scented steam.

"Still, what that little girl said about McNeal worries me. Seemed to worry those cops, too."

"You mean about hurting *another* animal? Yeah, that gave me a chill, too. I'm not a psychologist or a profiler, but that kid likes hurting others way too much. That's never a good thing."

She'd been worried that the ground would be too wet from the week-long rain, but the spot just under a graceful birch on the edge of the small wood was perfect. Mo unrolled her cushioned mat, settled her back against the smooth trunk, opened her netbook and started to read. Sure, it would be easier to read on her desk computer, but seven days of gray skies and rain had her going stir-crazy. Domino was good company and his antics were a hoot, but she needed to be *out*. It was comforting here, under the arching branches, surrounded with blooming wildflowers. There seemed to be even more of them than before. New growth sprouted everywhere, encouraged by the rains. She wasn't alone in enjoying the patch of flowers, either. Small birds and the park's semi-tame squirrels foraged for bugs and seeds under the cover of the leaves. Who was she kidding? She wasn't going to be able to read on a day like this. Leaning back, she savored the warm sun and rich scents swirling around her like an embrace.

Not far away, a group of kids stood, their banter and laughter adding to the pleasant atmosphere. Among them, she recognized the girl who had helped her rescue Domino. She really ought to tell her how it turned out, that the scruffy little cat was making his home with her now. Later, though. Right now, she couldn't muster the energy to hoist herself up and walk over. Listening to the happy talk and the bees droning in the blossoms, her eyelids grew heavier — until:

"McNeal, no one wants your kind of shit around here today."

Suddenly alert, Mo sat up and looked in the direction of the words. Jimmy McNeal was standing on the path facing the group of previously chattering kids. She'd heard the term stonewall before and now she was seeing a physical example of it. The small group had tightened their ranks and all stood facing the gangly bully with uniform expressions of disgust and anger. The girl Mo recognized stood slightly in front of them with arms folded. She said, "Just turn around and head back the way you came."

Off-balance at the reception, McNeal said, "Hey! What's the problem? I didn't do nothin'."

"Yet," the girl said. "But it always happens and we don't want to mess with it. C'mon, guys, let's get out of here."

As one, the kids turned and walked away from him, leaving him standing open-mouthed staring after them. Mo mentally applauded them as they strode away from him, but then, the girl looked back and tossed over her shoulder, "You know, that lady is right. It must be really awful to live with all that hate and anger all the time."

Oops. The repeat of the words he'd only heard from Mo broke the spell. Even from her distance, she could see rage fill him. Face locked in a snarl, his eyes sought Mo out. He jammed his hand into is pocket and started toward her.

Belatedly, the girl realized her mistake. She and the other kids froze in horror, eyes locked on McNeal.

Heart racing, Mo tightened her grip on her cane and stood. Facing him, she squared her shoulders and prayed she didn't look as nervous as she was.

"Hey! Bitch," he shouted at her. Quickening his pace, he left the path and plowed into the wildflowers. Suddenly, a small furry body exploded from the vegetation right in front of him. McNeal fell backward with a yell as the animal, a squirrel, ran up, over him and scrambled into the overhanging branches of the trees, shrieking and chittering in alarm.

There was a beat of silence, broken only by the frantic cries of the squirrel, then the clot of kids burst out laughing.

McNeal jumped to his feet and shot Mo a look of pure murder, then turned on his heel and ran away.

###

The dame's rocket was in full glory. So what if it was considered an invasive species? The lavender blossoms against the Queen Anne's lace, yarrow, coreopsis and other late spring blooms were beautiful in the afternoon sun. Mo settled herself on the bench at the edge of the fragrant sea of color and pulled her netbook from her shoulder bag. A book she'd been waiting for had just been released and she'd downloaded it into her e-reader program for a treat after her afternoon walk. Considering the four laps she'd just made, she figured she deserved a taste of it right then and there. She opened the little computer and lost herself in the story.

It was getting hard to see the print on the screen. Looking up, she realized with a shock that she'd been reading for hours and the setting sun cast long shadows over the deserted park. Chuckling at herself, she shut the system down and sat back, enjoying the evening breeze and the lovely colors the sunset painted across the sky. The night scent of the wildflowers surrounding the bench rose in a heady cloud. She felt safe and content.

She watched as the moon rose and the stars became visible. Around the park, the light-sensing lamps winked on, their rose-gold glow splashing warm ovals on the walking path turned silver in the moonlight. The temperature was rapidly dropping, too. She'd dressed for the warmth of the day, not the cool of the night. Beautiful sky or not, she needed to get home. Dropping the mini-computer into her bag, she levered herself off the bench with her cane.

"Thanks. That'll make it easier to carry. Hand it over."

McNeal stood a few yards away. Moonlight gleamed off the blade of a knife in his hand. She hadn't seen him in weeks, not since the day he ran off after being laughed at. She'd put him out of her mind, written him off — that was a mistake, it seemed. Abruptly, the emptiness of the park pressed home on her. Without warning, he lunged, and pain blossomed along a line across the bare forearm she'd clutched over the bag. She screamed.

Snarling, he shoved her, sending her sprawling, making her lose her hold on the bag which skittered into the shadows of the undergrowth. McNeal advanced, knife poised to cut again and anger welled up in her. No. This will *not* happen. Her hand closed on her cane. Instinct guided it up and around. Fury fueled the blow as she lashed him across the face making him stagger and fall. Before she realized what she was doing, she was scrambling up, climbing hand over hand up the aluminum shaft.

McNeal picked himself up, still clutching the knife. She didn't need to see his face to know it was contorted with animal rage.

She swung again. The force of the blow bent the already abused aluminum into a useless V, but she managed to knock him down again. This time he lost hold of the knife. It spun away, glinting faintly in the moonlight to vanish into a tall patch of dame's rocket.

Adrenaline lent her speed as she turned and sprinted away from him. The cinnamon scent of the flowers and a wild cursing rose behind her as McNeal tore at the patch to find the weapon. She focused on the copse before her. The embankment rose to street level just the other side of the stand of trees. A street lined with houses where she could call for help.

As she reached the dark mass of the hollies at the edge of the small wood, her foot caught on a bramble and she stumbled. *Come on, legs, hold out for a little while longer!*

Cursing, McNeal gave up the search for the knife and launched himself after her. "Damn you, I'll just break your neck with my bare hands."

He caught up with her at the edge of the trees, grasping fingers snagging her hair. Fear gave her a burst of speed, but as she dived aside, her punished legs finally gave way. She fell and tumbled through the stinging brambles and prickly hollies and found herself sprawled face down in a sun-dappled clearing. It was quiet, like the hush of a place just gone silent.

She struggled to her feet, then stopped. Sunlight? That was wrong. It was night when she ran into the trees. Steadying herself against the rough bark of a tree, she glanced wildly around. Where was the park? The copse wasn't that big, why couldn't she see the houses across the street? She became aware of the sound of someone crashing through the undergrowth as if it were at a distance.

"Goddammit, bitch! Where are you? I'll kill you. BITCH!" McNeal had followed her into the wood, but his words were barely reaching her, even though she knew he was shouting.

She turned to run in the direction she hoped the street was in, but she tripped and landed in a heap at the base of a huge, old oak. Was this the oak at the center of the copse? Somehow it looked larger, older. The crashing and the cursing were getting closer. Running into the trees had been a bid for safety, a way to throw McNeal off her track and give her time to reach someplace to call for help. It was a bid that would backfire on her if she couldn't get to her feet. A fallen branch lay on the mossy ground not far from her hand. It looked sturdy and just about the right length for a walking stick. Grabbing it, she pulled herself up and limped away from the crashing and swearing.

The swearing abruptly turned to screams. She froze in place, torn by the urge to flee danger and compassion for another human in distress. The screams grew more and more frantic, rising in pitch until they became one sustained note that held all the primal fear of humankind — then silence. She stood, clutching her oak stick for long moments, then crept slowly and cautiously in the direction she'd heard the screams. One by one, birds high in the branches took up their song. Insects buzzed in the air and among the wildflowers. A short distance away from the massive oak, she found a place where the leaf-strewn floor was churned up as if from a struggle. Something in the ivy growing up the side of an ancient alder caught her eye. A scrap of denim like the fabric of the boy's jacket was wedged between the thick vines.

Suddenly afraid, she looked around, but there was no sign of her former attacker. No sign of anything other than trees and dappled sunlight. Still, panic rose and she hurried away, faster and faster until, her legs gave way again and she fell, rolling and tumbling back into the night.

"There she is!" a man's voice called.

Oh no. Panic caught her breath in her throat. She clawed frantically for the oak branch, but it was a woman who called next, "Ms. McKinney?"

Through vision narrowed by fear, she slowly realized that there were blue and red flashing lights reflecting off of the trees. A woman in uniform hurried over to her, calling, "Ms. McKinney! It's Officer Rowan Wicks. Are you OK?"

Relief turned her muscles to jelly. She sat down hard

amid the trampled wildflowers, the rough oak staff clutched tight in her hands.

The policewoman knelt at her side. "We got a report of a disturbance in the park. A woman screaming and a man threatening. We found your purse and the neighbors said you'd been—" She spotted the gash on Mo's arm. "Hey! Bishop! Think I see where the blood on that knife came from. We need some first aid here!"

Mo tried to speak, but was shaking too hard to form words. Even when the EMTs came and helped her to the back of the waiting ambulance, all she could manage was a few whimpers. They sat her down and went to work: one gave her sips of water from a cup and draped a blanket around her shoulders while the other cleaned her slashed arm.

The policewoman stayed by her side while her partner went over to address a small group of people standing on the embankment. Mo recognized them as the residents of the row of neatly-kept Victorian houses facing the park. They must have been the ones who called the police. She was glad they were watching out. She couldn't hear the policeman's words, but she caught the sigh of relief from the group and the murmur of concerned voices.

Officer Wicks pulled her fuzzy focus back, asking, "Did you get a good look at whoever did this?"

Mo swallowed hard, tried to nod, but only managed a brief jerk. "McNeal. It was Jimmy McNeal." Her voice sounded harsh and strange to her ears. The EMT gave her another sip of water. It helped a little.

Wicks frowned and made a note on her pad.

Mo continued, "I'd been reading on the bench and lost track of time. When I got up to go home, he was there. He had a knife. I tried to run through the trees but—" Fear overwhelmed her again and she broke down in sobs.

The EMT who had been cleaning the wound looked up at her. "This is pretty deep, it'll need stitching. We better head for the hospital."

Mo was alarmed. "Hospital? NO!"

A hand lightly touched her shoulder. Officer Wicks said, "Don't worry, I'll ride with you. Bishop can follow in the cruiser."

Mo wanted to refuse, but the sting in her arm was settling into an insistent throb. Knowing there was no other way, she acquiesced reluctantly.

Shock set in, making the ride to the hospital and the route to the examination room a blur. She'd tried to answer their questions as best she could, but she didn't have a lot to offer. She didn't mention the forest. She couldn't. They'd slap her into a padded room so fast it would make her head spin. Maybe that's where she belonged, though. The forest had to have been some sort of hallucination, a waking dream brought on by fear. A primal safe place where the evil things of the world weren't welcome.

When the doctors had gone, leaving her with a long row of stitches swathed in bandage, making her look like she was wearing one white evening glove, the two officers came in and sat on either side of her. After a moment, Mo realized Wicks was talking to her. It was an effort to listen.

"That's some kind of cudgel you've got there. May I see it?"

Mo gaped at the stick in her hand almost as if seeing it the first time. "Oh. I hadn't even realized I still had it. I found it at the base of the big oak there in the park. I-I broke my cane when McNeal attacked me."

Wicks nodded, turning the branch in her hands. "We found it not far from the knife. Bent all to hell and gone. That must have been a helluva struggle." The policewoman handed the stick back with a genuine smile. "That's a beautiful length of oak. Lots of character in the wood. My mom would go nuts over it — she's Wiccan. Says oak is protective and a giver of strength. Whether you're Wiccan or not, it still makes a good walking stick."

Bishop still had his notebook open and his pen ready. He asked, "So you have no idea where McNeal went?"

"None," she said. A shudder wracked her. "I wish I did. It's terrifying to know he's still out there. I lost track of him after I fell through the undergrowth."

He nodded solemnly. "I don't blame you, Ms. McKinney, but we've got everyone on the look out for him. If he shows up, we'll find him."

"You can count on it." Wicks stood. "Well, let's get you home. You're probably ready to drop."

Mo spent the next weeks working the oak stick. She'd never done anything like that before, but when Officer Wicks mentioned the idea, it took hold. She was glad she had, too. The work was surprisingly relaxing and therapeutic. It also kept her mind off the fact that the stitches were itching like the devil. Domino had even enjoyed the process — well, he enjoyed having pitched battles with the curled shavings, anyway.

As she left the house, the heft and smooth, rich wood of her new walking stick felt comforting under her hand. She really hoped that the policewoman's mother was right about oak imparting strength and protection. She was going to need all she could get as she walked to the park for the first time since the attack. It was early morning and the place should be empty. She didn't know if that was a good thing or not. Shauna offered to go with her, but it was time to deal with her fear and that was something she had to do alone.

Summer was fast approaching and the trees and plantings had lost their early spring brightness and settled into a richer, darker green. Different flowers bloomed and she paused several times to enjoy the flame-bright wall flowers and graceful wisteria along the path. Small noises still made her jump and, when two dogs tore across the walk, she nearly had heart failure.

She wished they'd found McNeal, but they hadn't. Wicks and Bishop stopped by every couple days to let her know the progress of the hunt. They were puzzled that he hadn't turned up. No one had seen him, not even at the foster home where he'd been living.

On her second lap around the walking path, she stopped and looked at the copse. The places where McNeal ripped the dame's rocket out of the ground were already healing. New green shoots poked through the raw brown dirt. Soon it would be impossible to see the damage.

That was the way with life: it healed itself. She hoped that she would heal just as surely.

Now for the part she was really dreading — to address the hallucination of the forest. Too bad. It was *such* a lovely hallucination. Squaring her shoulders, she strode into the trees and stood in the middle next to the gnarled oak. Through the tangle of bramble and holly, she could see the embankment and beyond that, the row of houses with their gingerbread porches.

"See, Mo. Batshit bonkers," she murmured, turning to walk back into the park. "There is no for—"

Where a few moments before, there had been a small, overgrown stand of trees, she now looked into the depths of a lush, primal forest. As she stepped farther in, the light changed from the pale of just-morning to the richer hue of a setting sun. She took a couple slow steps forward in confusion and wonderment. The sky, where it was visible through the dense canopy was stained purple and rose and the sun's dying rays sent shadows across the mossy ground in the wrong direction. She whirled to look behind her. Trees stretched as far as she could see. It was as if the park were an almost forgotten memory. She reached out to touch the gnarled, central oak. At least she assumed it was the center of this wood as it formed the center of the small copse in her park. This seemed to be a *version* of the copse she was used to walking past, but somehow . . . older . . . .

I'm not afraid. Why am I not afraid?

Kneeling at the base of the oak, she found where she had fallen, where she had picked up the branch she was now using as a walking stick. Here, like the wildflower patch, the wounds were healing themselves. Looking closely, she could follow her path to the point where she originally fell into the wood. It was nowhere near an edge or a clearing. She then followed her tracks to where she'd gone to investigate the screams. The huge, ivy-covered alder was there. She looked for the denim scrap, but there was no sign of it.

Mo turned away in puzzlement, but as she did, the fading light played tricks on her, making the boles and bulges in the bark look like a human form. Stepping back, she cocked her head and squinted a little. Yeah, it looked like a leg emerging from that root and there was an arm . . . a shoulder . . . a face. . . .

Her heart skipped a beat. No. That was impossible. But was it any more impossible than a hidden forest? Moving around, she took a closer look and recoiled with a gasp. It was a face and it was one she knew. It was the face that had been haunting her nightmares, only here it was McNeal's mouth open in a soundless scream of terror. She stared, immobilized with horror, then turned to rush away — only to find herself on the edge of the thicket blinking in early morning sunlight.

"God. Oh, god. That was . . . I have to tell the police. . . ," she gasped, then stopped and slowly looked back. Back through the summer greenery to the Victorian houses facing the park. Tell the police what? That a tree in a mystical disappearing forest ate McNeal? Oh suuuuure.

She lowered herself onto the bench and sat back, eyes closed breathing deeply of the scent of the wildflower patch. Her pounding heart slowed and her racing thoughts snapped into focus. Wait. What was she so upset about? Hadn't the copse done what she was wanting the police and courts to do? It had protected her. Helped her. Okay, it wasn't how she'd imagined the problem being solved, nonetheless, it was solved. Jimmy McNeal would never hurt anyone again.

Across the way, a van pulled into the gravel lot. Doors opened, spilling out kids who ran in a happy, shrieking mass toward the play set. She sat and watched them play for a few moments, then turned back toward the copse. The leaves rustled gently in the early morning breeze.

She nodded, took a firmer grip on her walking stick and started home.

River Ghosts
by Dirk Griffin

river ghosts
guard the darkness
i see them keeping
watch about shores
in early light or new
twilight's haze

they speak fear
to weaker hearts

Elvis Returns

by Joanna Foreman

Officer Otis McCutcheon was the new guy. He'd been on the Indiana State Police Force for one year, and because no other recruits had been added to his unit, his fellow officers referred him as the rookie.

"Hey, Rookie, you seen Elvis yet?" J. D. Bullock, a tall, balding officer with a desk job and a pot belly to match, asked him one Friday morning at the station. Otis had been on his assignment three weeks at the time and had no idea what Bullock was talking about, so he took the bait, "What . . . Presley?"

The other officers snickered; J. D. Bullock guffawed and beat his fists on his desk so hard a glass of iced tea tipped over onto his blotter.

Otis bit his tongue and threw Bullock a look of disgust. He knew the harassment from his co-workers was harmless enough, and he wouldn't always be the new guy. After his shifts, he returned to his little log cottage in Brown County where his wife, Lucia, smothered him with all kinds of attention. Otis, in his blue uniform, all pressed and well fitting.

"Oh, Otis," she would say. "You look so good in that outfit." Why she called it an outfit he could not understand, although he knew that's the way women referred to their own clothes. It was a uniform, not an outfit. A Smokey the Bear uniform. Pants perfectly creased in front, the color of a gray-blue sky with dark blue stripes down each side seam. The shirt was a darker blue, shoulder flaps attached at the neckline with gold buttons; two pleated breast pockets, matching thread sewn along the edges; and his gold officer's badge placed just above the left shirt pocket. The triangular shape of the Indiana State Police decal rested proudly on his right shirt sleeve.

Every morning Otis groomed himself in front of the full-length mirror attached to the bathroom door. He knew he looked better than any other cop on the force. The others were too short or too tall, or overweight, or had any number of other physical detractions. Otis was just right at 5'10", weighing in at 165 lbs. He worked out at a local gym in Columbus three times a week — his abs hard and wavy — especially stunning in his Smokey suit.

Otis had Interstate 65 duty all the way from Jackson County at the Seymour exit number fifty, to north of Columbus, exit seventy-three. He saw it as twenty-three boring miles up and down, all day long. When an emergency call came from anywhere else, say State Highway 46, or even better, Federal 31, Otis wasn't called upon to answer because he had to stay right alongside the Interstate in case there were any emergencies. And there had been a few calls, but when they came in, the other officers converged on the scene en masse, leaving Otis to feel like a fifth wheel every time. So, most days he pulled his patrol car off the road into a clump of evergreen bushes and aimed his radar gun. "Gotcha!" he'd say, and ease back onto the pavement, speed up, flip the switch to activate his lights and siren. The speeders never knew where he'd come from. He held the record for speeding tickets that year.

Otis' assignment changed to the night shift, which he expected to be even more lackluster. Absolutely nothing exciting happened along I-65 during the wee dark night hours. No one was speeding at night. How could they when the Interstate was packed with trucks, Peterbilt rigs, cruising two-by-two? Otis loved to eavesdrop as the truckers conversed over their radios. He knew them all by name: Big Purple Peter, Dream Catcher, Mamma's Toy, and Soul Searcher. He moved around the channels at night to pick up the most intriguing conversations between the drivers. Someday he'd write a book, he thought.

Just past midnight on Otis' first night on late shift, he saw a bright red Ford, possibly a vintage 1968 Mustang model, parked alongside the shoulder at mile marker fifty-three, right past the White River Bridge. He parked his cruiser behind it and aimed a spotlight into the rear of the vehicle. It appeared empty, but Otis had learned appearances could be deceiving. He activated his video cam, slid out of his seat, and walked up to the passenger side. He directed his flashlight inside and saw no one. Otis tried the doors but they were locked. The pristine condition of the interior, along with the well-maintained exterior, assured Otis the owner would return soon. He noted the license plate, make and model, and called in to see if it might be a stolen vehicle, but it was clean. Otis placed a day-glow orange warning sticker on the windshield: Move it in seventy-two hours or we tow.

Otis reentered the highway and drove along, thinking nothing more of it. People left their cars alongside the Interstate roads all the time. They ran out of gas, or broke down for other reasons. Sometimes it took them a day or two to return, occasionally to find their car on four concrete blocks, but that was not his problem. He wasn't the world's babysitter.

Otis was on duty four nights, and off three, so the following week after being off, he was patrolling his stretch of road around midnight, and up ahead he saw the same vehicle at the exact location it had been previously. He pulled over and once again gave it a thorough check. It was just as before, except the orange sticker had been removed. He called in the license number to double check, but unsurprisingly the results showed nothing out of the ordinary. He reported it in as an abandoned vehicle and made arrangements with Tommy's Towing to remove it. He applied another warning sticker and drove off.

The next morning, a Friday, he went into the station to retrieve his weekly paycheck. J. D. Bullock sat at his desk, same old blotter but a fresh glass of tea. He was viewing the video cam from Otis' previous weeks' pullovers.

"Tommy's Towing says you owe him one. Your *alleged* mustang was gone when they arrived," Bullock said.

"Yeah?" replied Otis, "I guess the owner finally came and got it. Immaculate, vintage 1968 Ford Mustang." The grin on Bullock's face told Otis something was up. Otis thought Bullock should never play poker with anyone but a blind man.

"So, Rookie, have you seen Elvis yet?" asked Bullock.

"Get off my back, J.D.," Otis said.

J. D. snickered, and a few other officers cackled and chortled, and Otis could hear them saying something about Elvis as the office door slammed shut behind him and he headed to his patrol car. *Forget them*, he thought.

He drove through Brown County and up the winding road to his little cabin, where he expected Lucia to be awaiting him with open arms. She had baked an apple pie and the aroma wafted through the opened front windows. He decided he'd have some for breakfast, along with the sausage patties and fried eggs she probably had ready for him. She didn't care what he ate, as long as he kept that uniform on. She sometimes made him wear it to bed, which he gladly did. Otis had heard that cops' wives are born, not made, and Lucia McCutcheon was his prize.

No sooner had he opened the cabin door, he saw Lucia standing at their bedroom doorway, wiggling her index finger back and forth.

"Come here, Otis, I have a new little something to show you."

Apple pie forgotten, Otis hoped she had ordered from the Victoria Secret catalog he had left lying on her vanity with the page opened, the corner turned down to a black, lacy camisole. He had imagined her in it already. He strutted to the bedroom. He would wear his outfit and she would wear hers.

Pair of Normal What?

The next couple of nights Otis drove Interstate 65 as usual, and at approximately three in the morning he would pass mile marker fifty-three. He halfway expected the Ford to be there, but it wasn't.

A few nights later along the dark stretch of highway, the red Mustang was parked, again void of its orange sticker. Otis rubbed his eyes and quickly pulled his patrol car off to the side. What in the world was going on? Had his mind been on that black camisole and he hadn't noticed the car those past couple of nights? Why on God's green earth would anyone abandon such a beautiful car? He called in the license number, make and model. He felt foolish repeating this procedure, but it was required.

This time he examined the name of the owner: Wyatt E. Davis. *Nothing unusual about that, but here's something I hadn't noticed before*, Otis thought. *The license plate hasn't been updated from 1968. Well . . . that just has to be a mistake! It would have showed up previously when I called it in, wouldn't it?*

He got out of his patrol car to place another sticker on the windshield. When he opened his driver's door to get back in, he heard the familiar voice of a trucker. Soul Searcher was calling him on the CB. "Come in, big buddy."

Otis grabbed his CB radio. "In, Soul Searcher. Over."

You at this spot every night. You got a problem? Over."

"Ten-Four. Only around midnight. That's when this old Mustang shows up. You know anything about it? Over."

"Ten-Four. You know about Elvis?"

Otis' breath caught in his throat. "That's a negative, Soul Searcher. Over."

"Thought you might need some help with that, you being the new guy and all. Meet me up at the truck stop, next exit. Buy me a coffee. I'll fill you in. Over."

"That's a Big Ten-Four. Over."

Otis drove the five miles to the next exit with his mind full of questions. What does this Elvis fellow have to do with an abandoned vehicle? And why did he continue to bring it back to the same place, night after night? Was a drug deal involved? If so, maybe he could nab the guy and make a name for himself. He hoped Soul Searcher could enlighten him, and the guys back at the station would finally quit pestering him about Elvis. He also considered the possibility that this was a joke the guys were playing on him, and Soul Searcher was part of their nefarious plot.

The two men sat at the bar at Sammy's Truck Stop. The waitress had a cute little white apron tied around her tiny waist. She poured hot coffee into mugs and brought them warm cherry pie with vanilla ice cream. Otis watched her walk away and briefly contemplated how she would look in Lucia's black camisole.

"What I've heard through the years is this," Soul Searcher said. "Back then, White River and the local creeks flooded during the heavy rains of spring. Of course the flooding causes no problem along the Interstate now, since drainage channels were installed years ago. Wyatt Elvis Davis was a traveling salesman. Got that fancy new Ford back in '68, but only had it a week or two when he lost control and went over the bridge. Dang thing landed on its roof and flattened it so bad no way his body could have got out, but he was never found. Some say his ghost comes around midnight to visit that car he loved."

Pajr of Nomal What?

Otis felt a shiver run through his body. He had heard plenty of ghost stories when he was a kid, but thought they were all hogwash. Until now. He thanked Soul Searcher, paid the bill, left a generous tip for the waitress and went on his way.

When Otis' shift ended in the morning, he went straight to Headquarters and into the computer room where all the files were kept. He asked Donna, the unit's secretary, to check out the accident reports.

"Thirty-eight years back would be in the archives, Otis. I'll have to dig it out. I'll have it for you tomorrow," she said.

The next morning he arrived early, as soon as his night shift ended, waiting for Donna. He circled her desk, jiggling the keys on his belt, and wondered when she was going to finally drag herself into the office. No one seemed to be paying attention to him, so he took a seat in Donna's chair, leaned over her desk and sorted through the paperwork. There it was, a manila envelope with the name Otis McCutcheon printed on it. Exactly what he'd ordered!

He slit the envelope with his pocket knife and pulled out two sheets of paper and began to read: Wyatt Elvis Davis, born April 2, 1945, age twenty-three, had lost control of his car at mile marker fifty-three during the spring flooding. The flooded Interstate had been closed for hours; Elvis had either ignored or had not seen the warning signs, driven on into deep water and hydroplaned. His brand new Ford flipped and landed, just like Soul Searcher said, upside down, flat as a pancake, on the bank of the swollen White River below. An old newspaper clipping in black and white of the upside-down car was attached to the report. Donna had done good work, Otis thought. The article said the man's body was presumed to have been thrown from the car and swept

64

downstream in the raging current, although how it could have escaped from the vehicle was a mystery. The accident happened just after midnight. Heroic efforts to locate Elvis continued for two weeks; his body was never found.

J. D. Bullock had been watching Otis out of the corner of his eye. He marched himself over to Donna's desk. "You see it now, boy?"

"I get it, J.D. I get it. *Now* I've seen Elvis. I'm a believer . . . maybe now you'll leave me alone?"

Officer Bullock laughed, slapped Otis on the back, and went back to his desk. "Oh, by the way, a new recruit is coming end of the week. You need to show him the ropes. We're gonna move you to Federal 31, day shift."

Otis grinned and took the manila envelope, put it into the glove box of his patrol car, and drove home to Lucia.

On Friday the new recruit, Billy Dunham, showed up and rode along with Otis for the next three weeks. Otis made sure they cruised past mile marker fifty-three at midnight, but he didn't say a word about the Ford alongside the road. Curiously, Billy sat quietly in the passenger seat and did not ask Otis why he didn't pull over. Otis wondered if it was possible Billy wasn't observant enough to see the Mustang.

Billy was assigned his own patrol car and Otis began his new route — Federal 31. The dayshift guys all hung out before duty at Seymour Coffee & Donuts and speculated about Billy. When would he call in the make, model and license of Elvis's vehicle? He'd been patrolling around midnight in that area for ten days and still hadn't called in a report. Surely he'd noticed the car by now!

Finally, Otis couldn't take it any longer. "You seen Elvis yet?" he asked Billy one payday morning at the station.

Billy slowly turned his gaze toward Otis and sneered, but said nothing.

A creepy feeling came over Otis and he couldn't get out of the room fast enough. Next day at the donut shop he told the other guys about it. They scratched their heads and tried to figure out why the rookie wasn't playing the game.

A week later Office Bullock, famous for his silly grin, asked Billy, "You seen Elvis yet, Rookie?" Billy stared precisely at Bullock; the chilly look he gave him wiped the stupid smirk right off. The other guys saw it but pretended not to.

Billy was the number one topic of conversation for the next couple of months, not only at the donut shop, but whenever he wasn't around. The guys couldn't figure it out, and it was driving them to distraction. No one even knew where he lived. The only information they had was his full name, DOB and SSN. Bullock told them to forget it, that Billy was a regular guy who appreciated vintage Mustangs. He told the men to get their minds on their work. But they wouldn't leave it alone. They finally had someone follow Billy to make sure he was on the route at the given time. Sure enough, he was, and a few times he drove onto the highway shoulder, behind the Ford. But he never called it in. It was almost as though he stopped to get a look at it and then went on his way.

Otis came up with the idea to have a secret video cam installed in Billy's patrol car so they could keep an eye on him. Turned out, he parked behind that car every night for five minutes or so. Sometimes he'd get out and walk up to the car, open the door and sit in it for a while. Otis wondered why he hadn't thought of that. What a thrill it would have been to experience the interior of a 1968 Mustang, to caress the vinyl seat, take hold of the smooth, wood-grained steering wheel, maybe even turn on the radio. Then he remembered — the doors had been locked!

Billy Dunham, sure enough, wasn't following proper police procedure, and Officer Bullock knew his Captain would want to follow up on it when he got wind of Billy's unusual behavior. He thought he'd get a jump on it, so he called Indiana State Police Headquarters with an inquiry about their unit's newest rookie, the one who had been on the job not more than three months, William Edward Dunham. He requested detailed information: the officer's history, academy training, and current address. He was informed the data would be forthcoming in a facsimile report.

The instant the fax machine rang, the officers on duty tripped over one another to see what it would spit out.

> *There is no record of a William Edward Dunham. He does not exist in our computer system, either as a new or retired recruit. The last officer assigned to your unit was Otis McCutcheon. No other officers have been dispensed from then until this date.*

Otis and Bullock double-checked what records they had of Billy, and they watched those secret tapes over and over. Otis was the first one to figure it out. He hadn't paid attention to Billy's full name before, William Edward Dunham born April 2, 1985. Just like Wyatt Elvis Davis, born April 2, 1945. Born on the same day, forty years apart, same initials, which could have been coincidence, but the Social Security number was the same for each man!

Elvis Returns was originally published in Ghostly Hauntings of Interstate 65.

Coyote

by Dirk Grffin

how you tricked
me laughing
at my loss

you promised
but lied in the
same words

and still i believe
you can be trusted

even though
tricks are your trade

C. S. Lewis and Pleasure Riding

by Janet Wolanin Alexander

Trail riding took on a whole new dimension after I read *The Chronicles of Narnia* by C.S. Lewis last summer. The seven-book, pre-Harry Potter series, written in England between 1939 and 1956, records the adventures of several British children in a world populated by talking animals and mythological creatures.

How exactly was my horseback riding affected? My imagination was activated! My horse Highlander and I morphed into a Centaur and explored our magic kingdom, a state forest in southeastern Indiana. The maples, oaks, hickories, and tulip poplars became giant broccoli plants. Holes in the trunks were the homes of gnomes. Spider webs strung across the trail were "no trespassing" barricades. Biting deerflies were military patrol squadrons enforcing the arachnids' warnings. The loud droning of cicadas was an orchestra of dentists drilling their patients' teeth. The song of the wood thrush transposed into the fluid notes of a flute. A scattering of mushrooms with flat, bright yellow tops, doubled as empty bar tables in a closed cafe. The blossoms of Queen Ann's Lace in the adjoining field were their tatted tablecloths laid out to dry. The thistle flowers next to them, from which fritillary butterflies greedily guzzled nectar, were magenta goblets. . . .

One day the following May, Highlander and I were innocently trotting down the trail when crazed caterpillars, suspended on silk strands from the branches overhead, tried

Pair of Normal What?

to strangle us. As we passed, the gauntlet of invertebrate trapeze artists, lassoers, and bungee jumpers dropped upon us. They tried to knit our top and bottom eyelashes together and to sew our nostrils and mouths shut. Biting larvae landed on my neck and tried to inch their way down my shirt. I frantically tried to claw them and their silk off before Highlander and I were anesthetized and mummified alive. . . .

My favorite books in the *Chronicles* are *The Magician's Nephew* and *A Horse and His Boy* because, of course, they feature horses. In the latter, which should be co-titled *A Mare and Her Girl*, a boy and a girl flee a hostile country on Narnian horses. I smiled when the boy's horse gives him riding lessons; laughed when he, forced at one point to ride an ordinary horse, comes to fully appreciate his talking mount; and concurred with the pacing advice the horse gives him during their long distance endurance ride.

My favorite passage in the series, however, occurs in the first and most well-known book, *The Lion, The Witch and The Wardrobe,* when Aslan, the lion/creator of Narnia, takes two girls on a ride. The resulting flight of fancy weaves equine and feline imageries into pure whimsical delight.

What fun it's been to have my imagination stimulated into overdrive by *The Chronicles*!

Because C.S. (Clive Staples) Lewis has helped me rediscover my inner child, I now enjoy riding in the C.S. (Clark State) Forest even more than before!

A longer version , "Reading C.S. Lewis Adds to the Pleasure of Trail Riding," was published in the September-October/2003 issue of The Trail Rider.

Deadly Relics
by Glenda Mills

It was the third death in as many weeks at St. Michael's parish.

The first had been Erma Becht, a middle-aged school teacher with two grown children, three grandchildren and no apparent reason to throw herself off the cliffs at the edge of town. The following week, Karen McCloud had come home from an evening parish council meeting to find her husband, David, in a pool of blood. His throat had been cut, and there was a knife lying beside his right hand. This morning, Father George had celebrated Mass for the third victim, Sean Williams, an honor student with a full athletic scholarship to the University of Kentucky basketball program. Days before, a family out for a walk had seen him wade into the Ohio River. By the time they realized he was in trouble, he had drowned. The first two had been ruled suicides, the last an accident. As the priest took off his chasuble and loosened the cincture on his alb, he thought about Sean, and Erma, and David. None of their deaths made sense. Assuming Erma had been suicidal, she was terrified of heights. She couldn't even get on a ladder at the church to help hang the Advent wreath. David grew faint at the sight of blood, and Sean, for all his athleticism, had never learned to swim. He didn't go into water, even in shallow areas. Aside from the deviations in personalities, the police could find no evidence of foul play, but Father George knew something was wrong. He just didn't know what.

###

Supper had come and gone, uneaten. "Hail Mary, full of grace, the Lord is with thee." The smooth beads sliding through his fingers, the gentle rhythm of the words, were just what Father George needed to ease his restless mind. Sean's funeral earlier that day was still too fresh for sleep to come easily. As a child, he'd gone to bed most nights clutching his rosary like a sacred teddy bear. His mother left when he was five, so he would imagine Mary tucking him in and kissing him good night. Other children's mothers read them bedtime stories; his prayed with him instead.

Somewhere between a Glory Be and an Our Father, he had dozed off. But now, with light filling the room and a deep voice like distant thunder calling his name, the priest was fully awake. A figure dressed in armor and carrying a sword and shield descended through the ceiling and stood at the side of his bed. The fog of drowsiness and terror that had filled his mind began to burn away with the dawning of realization. He knew angels could appear in human form, but he'd never expected St. Michael the Archangel to look like he did on his prayer card. The image was exact, except on his prayer card he wasn't holding the mane of the severed head of a lion in his hand. For a moment that seemed to last an eternity, the priest and the angel looked at each other, and then the vision ended. There was no dramatic exit, no ascension through the ceiling this time. The heavenly messenger simply vanished.

Since there was no chance of sleep now, the priest got up, made a pot of coffee, and pulled the Bible concordance off his book shelf. Once again, he prayed for wisdom, guidance and discernment.

The first thing he looked for was the word lion. Soon he found 1 Peter 5:8 and read, "Be sober and vigilant. Your

Pajr of Normal What?

opponent the devil is prowling around like a roaring lion looking for someone to devour." His mind began to race. Surely the Devil, Lucifer himself, wasn't actually in his parish. Maybe the police had missed something. Maybe there was a serial killer in the town. The reference had to be a way of saying that evil things were happening, a way of confirming his earlier suspicions that something was wrong. Satan was at work in the lives of his parishioners. What he didn't know yet was exactly how they were being attacked and who was doing the attacking.

###

"Father, you don't look well. Is something wrong?" Clara, the church secretary, had walked into his office to bring him some checks to sign.

"Long day followed by a longer night."

"I know what you mean. With all the horrible things that have been going on lately, I don't think any of us are at ease these days. Is there anything I can get you?"

"Is there fresh coffee?"

"I put some on when I first got here. It should be ready by now. I'll get you a cup."

"Thanks."

Clara returned within minutes. Father George was just finishing the last signature. "Perfect timing, as usual," he said, taking the coffee mug from her. As she pulled her hand away from the cup, he noticed a large ring he'd never seen her wear before. It was a large, amethyst stone with a lion's head engraved on the face of it. "Clara, is that new?"

"I've had it for a month or so. This is the first time I've worn it to work. Do you like it?"

"I have to admit it's quite unusual. Where did you get it?"

Pair of Normal What?

Clara paused, looked out the window for a moment, and then said quietly, "I have a confession to make. I got it from the guy in the parking lot, the one you ran off. I know it's probably just a cheap trinket, and I know how angry you were that he was selling stuff without permission. In my defense, I didn't realize he was a trespasser until after I made my purchase."

The priest smiled. "Even though this isn't an official confession, consider yourself forgiven." Clara opened her mouth to say something else, but before she could utter a syllable, the phone rang. She turned and walked quickly out of the office and down the hall to answer it.

Father George looked at his now empty desktop and thought back to the vendor in the parking lot. Clara was right. It had been about a month ago. He had come out the back door of the church sacristy after 11:00 Mass with nothing on his mind but lunch. When he first saw the group of people huddled around the car in the parking lot, he'd figured it was just a social gathering. It wasn't until he got closer to the group that he noticed the man selling alleged relics and other sundry religious items out of the trunk of his car. The priest had approached the man and asked him to leave. He was, after all, on private property without permission. The man had refused, claiming he'd been invited by one of the parishioners to come and sell his items. An argument ensued, and as the man became more and more belligerent, Father George's temper reached its boiling point. He took the plastic container of merchandise, dumped it out on the ground, and announced to the gaping crowd and the stubborn peddler that if everyone wasn't off the grounds in five minutes, he was calling the police. He later apologized to the congregation for his outburst, but it had cleared the parking lot. Father George shook his head as he remembered his tirade. "Just like Jesus in the temple," he said to no one in particular, "driving out the money changers. Can't have St. Michael's become a den of thieves." The words were no sooner out of his mouth than one word began to echo in his brain. Thieves. Thieves. Thief. The thief. Suddenly, he remembered another verse about a thief. It was the teaching about Jesus being the good shepherd who, unlike the thief who comes to steal and slaughter and destroy, comes to bring abundant life. Once again, Father George thought of the Devil. Everything was leading him to the same chilling conclusion. He grabbed his jacket from the back of his chair, called down the hall to Clara that he was going out for a while, and ran out the door to his car.

Somehow, the pieces were falling into place. After he'd left the office, he'd gone to see Erma's husband, David's wife, Kathy, and Sean's parents. All of them confirmed his suspicions. Erma, David, and Sean had all bought lion rings from the man in the parking lot. The cursed chunks of metal and stone he now carried in his pocket were the instruments Satan had used to gain access to his flock. He thought he'd even figured out the strange deaths. The Devil had tempted Jesus by telling Him to throw Himself from the parapet of the temple. When the demons at Gadarene were cast out, they begged Jesus to send them into a herd of swine. The swine ran over a cliff and drowned. The demoniac at Capernaum lived among the tombs and used stones to bruise and cut himself. He had to get back to Clara. He had to find out how many more rings were out there and destroy them.

Pair of Normal What?

The smell of gasoline hit him as soon as he opened the door. As he turned the corner, he saw Clara sitting cross-legged on the floor in the hallway. Her hair clung to the sides of her face. Her clothes and the carpet around her were dark and wet. She had a lighter in her hand. There had been another story of a boy who was possessed. According to the boy's father, the demon caused the child to fall into fire.

"Clara, what are you doing?" The fumes from the gasoline were strong, and he fought back a cough.

"Clara isn't here, priest. Would you like to leave a message?" The voice was not Clara's. It wasn't even human. It was low and guttural, exactly what he would have imagined a voice from Hell would sound like. Clara's upper lip pulled back in an expression that was a cross between a sneer and a snarl.

Father George had no idea what to do next. He'd read through the rite of exorcism in seminary, but he'd never performed one. He'd never even seen one, except for the Hollywood version. This wasn't a movie, and if he didn't do something quickly, Clara was going to burn to death in front of him. He prayed the most frantic prayer of his life, begging God to do what he knew he could not do alone. Instinctively, he crossed himself and began, "St. Michael the Archangel, defend us in battle. Be our safeguard against the wickedness and snares of the devil."

The demon shrieked. "Don't try that shit with me. You don't have the balls. Where were you when I threw sweet Erma off the cliffs? Or when David was spewing blood from the slit in his throat? Or when that prick Sean's lungs were filling with water? You couldn't save them, and you can't save her."

"Rebuke him, O God, we humbly pray, and do thou, O prince of the Heavenly hosts, cast into Hell Satan and all the evil spirits who roam the world seeking the ruin of souls. Amen. In the name of Jesus, I command you to come out of her!"

Clara's head snapped back like she'd been struck in the face. For a moment, she was still, and Father George waited to see if the demon had truly gone. Then her head came forward, and her eyes stared back at him with fury. "You stupid asshole. Did you really think that would work? After I finish off your darling Clara, I'm coming for you. I'm going to enjoy using the shepherd to take out the rest of the flock."

The priest reached into his pocket and pulled out his rosary. He held the crucifix out in front of him. His hand was shaking and the beads clinked against each other like tiny wind chimes. "Our Father, Who art in Heaven, hallowed be thy name. Thy kingdom come, thy will be done on earth as it is in Heaven."

"Give us this day our daily bread, and forgive us our trespasses as we forgive those who trespass against us. . . ." There were two voices now, his and a child's. The priest stopped, but the child's voice, his voice when he was a boy, continued, "And lead us not into temptation, but deliver us from evil." A smile came across Clara's face. "Ever wonder where she is? You know you've thought about it. What kind of bitch leaves her son? If the whore who gave birth to you can't love you, how can your God love you?"

Tears welled up in Father George's eyes. He watched as Clara's countenance changed into that of a much younger woman with blue eyes and blond hair. He knew that face from the pictures his father had kept and from the faint memories of his childhood. "Mama?"

"Hey, Georgie," she said in a whispery voice with just a hint of a Tennessee mountain accent. She smiled and he smiled back. "I've missed you."

"I've missed you, too." Instinctively, he reached for her, completely focused on the illusion in front of him. She laughed, but soon the melodic sounds grew loud and raspy. He recoiled in horror as her cheeks sank in and her skin wrinkled, turned to dust and fell away. The skull's hollow eyes stared back at him. "She's mine, you know. She hung herself when you were just a snot-nosed brat. I can see by the stupid look on your face that you didn't know. She hated her little Georgie so much, her life was so miserable, that she chose to die rather than be your mommy. Sucks, huh?"

Father George's voice was eerily calm. "It's not true. You're a liar. She would never have killed herself."

"Well, you see, Georgie, normally you'd be right about me. I lie a lot. But this time, the truth is just so much more fun."

The surreal calmness shattered like glass around him. He remembered the people who had come by the house after his mom left, the sadness on their faces, his dad in his best suit dropping him off at the neighbor's house for a few hours. As he got older, he had wondered why his dad kept so many reminders of his mother around. Most people would have purged them out of anger and resentment, but he treasured them.

The avalanche of truth combined with years of pain and doubt drove him to his knees, and he sobbed. His body collapsed under the weight of his grief, and he lay there completely paralyzed by it. The demon was laughing. He could hear it, but it was distant, like the sound of a train whistle at the end of a long tunnel. He raised his head slightly from the rough nap of the carpet and once again saw Clara's face. The demon's laughter continued, but even as her mouth laughed, tears were running down her cheeks. The fury in her eyes was gone, replaced by fear and pleading. He had to help her. He tried desperately to remember the rite. "Lord, I can't do this without You. Please, for the sake of Your servant Clara, show me what to do."

Suddenly, on the office wall behind Clara's head, words began to form. He watched as the letters came together. It was as if a finger of fire was writing each syllable, etching them into the drywall. Father George stood up, made the sign of the cross, and began reading, "I adjure you, ancient serpent, by the judge of the living and the dead, by your Creator, by the Creator of the whole universe, by Him who has power to consign you to hell, to depart forthwith in fear, along with your savage minions, from this servant of God, Clara, who seeks refuge in the fold of the Church."

Clara's back arched and the demon's laughter became a howl of pain. The priest walked forward and traced the sign of the cross on the woman's forehead. Clara's hand grabbed his wrist. Her fingernails dug into his flesh and small trickles of blood converged into a stream on his arm and dripped from his fingertips. He swallowed a scream. "I adjure you again, not by my weakness but by the might of the Holy Spirit, to depart from this servant of God, Clara, whom almighty God has made in His image. Yield, therefore, yield not to my own person but to the minister of Christ. For it is the power of Christ that compels you, who brought you low by His cross. Tremble before the mighty arm that broke asunder the dark prison walls and led souls forth to light."

For the first time since this nightmare had begun, Clara's voice spoke to him. "Father, it's gone. I'm all right now.

You don't have to destroy the rings. It won't come back." She released her grip on his arm and her body relaxed. For a moment, he paused. Had he said anything about the rings in his pocket to Clara? No, he was sure he hadn't. He traced the sign of the cross on her chest and continued, "May the trembling that afflicts this human frame, the fear that afflicts this image of God descend on you." He traced a cross again on her forehead.

Clara's voice pleaded, "Father, stop. You're hurting me. Please, stop."

He continued, ignoring the voice that he now knew was not really Clara's. "Make no resistance nor delay in departing from this woman, for it has pleased Christ to dwell in man. Do not think of despising my command because you know me to be a great sinner. It is God Himself who commands you; the majestic Christ who commands you. God the Father commands you; God the Son commands you; God the Holy Spirit commands you." With each command, Father George traced a cross on Clara's forehead while the demon cursed and screamed obscenities. As he reached down to once again trace a cross on her chest and continue the prayer, the demon sank her teeth into his arm. It snarled and growled as it bit down harder and harder, desperately trying to keep him from touching her again.

Sweating from the struggle and wincing from the searing pain of the bite, he managed to trace the cross once again on her chest as he finished the prayer on the wall in front of him. "The faith of the holy apostles Peter and Paul and of all the saints commands you; the blood of the martyrs commands you; the continence of the confessors commands you; the devout prayers of all holy men and women command you; the saving mysteries of our Christian faith command you."

Clara's jaw released and Father George pulled away. Her body rose from the floor and jerked violently in mid air like a marionette being controlled with invisible strings. The demon screamed one last time before releasing his hold. Her body fell limp to the carpet. Exhausted, Father George leaned against the wall and slid down gently beside her. The words on the wall faded until there was no trace of their fiery presence. The gasoline had left a crimson rash on his secretary's exposed skin. Her eyes were puffy and red. She was wheezing and coughing. The fight over, he was once again cognizant of the deep wounds on his arm and wrist. Both of them needed medical attention. Clara stirred beside him and sat up. "Father, what happened?"

"Do you remember anything?"

"No, nothing. I was working at my desk. I heard someone come in, so I walked out in the hall to see who was here. After that, it's all a blank." She looked down at her wet clothes and sniffed the air. She saw the lighter still in her hand, threw it across the room, and looked back at Father George in wide-eyed panic.

He reached for her, and she collapsed into his shoulder, sobbing. "You're safe now, I promise. Everything's okay." As he pulled out his phone to dial 911, he wondered how in the world he could explain their conditions honestly without ending up in the psych ward for observation.

Agony and Ecstasy
by J. Baumgartle

My son and I
are at opposite poles
of what is said
and understood.
Our communication
is wrenched
from a painful antiphony
of blind guesses, labored
as that first turmoil
in which we struggled
for the same thing–
accomplished,
joyful as our merged cries.
No lack of love,
I never thought that.
We are used to
driving down the road
poised uneasily in
each other's consciousness,
on the way to Karate,
lessons *he* chose
—no more than
the usual disparity
in any male-female
exchange, with
left-brain to right-brain,
first-born to last-born
complications.

But to see you there, son,
barefoot, in black,
obeying some zero-G
directive from above—
I write, I know
this drive, this need
—a wordless muse
interpreting space
with leaded angles,
like the boughs of dogwood
you filled my arms with once. . . .
I wish we could as easily
function in this world,
submit that reverence
you do each other
and go on. . . .
Nothing you could ever
say or not say
would negate that integral
fourth-dimension awareness:
our other life, the real one,
where we know who we are.

Sense of Humor
by Marian Allen

Any time you hear Person A say that Person B has no sense of humor, it usually means Person B doesn't think Person A is funny.

Hoy Spencer used to say his cousin May Alice had no sense of humor.

"I'm just kidding around," he said, as a child. When he grew up, he said, "It's all in good fun."

From the time they were children, Hoy targeted his cousin with his wisecracks, half-witticisms, and practical jokes. Oh, how he loved practical jokes.

He was the boy who rang the doorbell and ran away. He was the boy who bought the hand-buzzer from the back pages of the comic books. He was the boy who gave May Alice a kaleidoscope that made a black ring around her eye the day before her First Communion.

May Alice, on the other hand, was born refined. She appreciated clever wordplay, elegant turns of phrase, odd juxtapositions, tumbling kittens — amusements that Hoy wouldn't have recognized as comical if they'd jumped in front of him and honked his nose.

May Alice responded to Hoy with tears, patience, courteous avoidance, and stoicism as she matured and Hoy grew.

Yes, any time you saw that twinkle in Hoy's eye, you knew you'd better check the cushions for whoopee bladders and the rug for plastic dog doo. If you tried to get him to leave his cousin alone, he would chuckle at you, and you figured you could expect a delivery of a dozen anchovy pizzas.

"I always did love to rattle May Alice's cage," he would say. "She never did have much of a sense of humor."

One October night in her 58th year, a stronger Hand than Hoy's rattled May Alice's cage and her spirit flew the coop. In other words, she died.

May Alice had arranged for a closed casket, but the lid and the wall behind it were covered with photographs from her life.

When Hoy walked in, the crowd parted for him. Fans of his humor whispered about how broken up he must be; partisans of May Alice muttered about his aggravation contributing to her early demise.

One way or the other, there was no denying there had been a connection between the cousins.

"Come on up here and look, Hoy." Great-Aunt Lily led him into the group around the coffin. "There's quite a few pictures of the two of you together."

Most of them showed his hand making devil-horns or "L" for "loser" above her head.

"I know how close the two of you were," Aunt Lily said uncertainly.

"help," said a small voice from inside the coffin. "help me. let me out."

Every jaw within hearing dropped. Every eye bugged out.

Aunt Lily gave Hoy a suspicious look. He blinked back at her innocently. She let go of his elbow and stepped away, as if tastelessness might be catching.

Cousin Edie, ever the lady, took a deep breath and set the tone of ignoring what everybody had just heard. "Here's the two of you at the river camp, where you made a sand cake and told May Alice it was chocolate with cinnamon on it. . . ."

"Let me out!" Now that Hoy was right up next to the casket, the voice was louder.

Great-Aunt Lily, who was nervous, started to cry. When her son came over to comfort her, she said, "Go get that funeral home man. Tell him to get in here. He's got to see about this."

"Let me out! Open this coffin! It's dark in here!"

The eye of every visitor — every scowling eye — fixed on the man now standing alone in front of the casket. Disapproval pulsed toward him like those curved lines from cartoon rayguns.

"Oh, my lord," Hoy said, "she's alive!"

"That ain't May Alice's voice." Uncle Benton flushed, embarrassed by what was happening, by what he was suggesting.

Cousin Edie poked Hoy in the arm and whispered. "That ain't funny, Hoy. Stop it right now. This ain't no Halloween party."

Hoy turned so pale he was almost blue. "I ain't doing it! Open up that coffin! She's still alive! She's just been playing possum!"

"Stop it, Hoy." Uncle Benton grabbed Hoy's arm and pulled him down the aisle. "Come on away from there."

"no, no, stay." The voice got softer as Hoy moved back into the room.

Mr. Stillman came rushing decorously in for an increasingly agitated conversation with the family. Hoy was brought forward, protesting his innocence. Still, every time he closed his mouth, that voice from the grave begged for freedom. Aunt Lily backhanded Hoy with her purse and threatened to spank him, big as he was.

Mr. Stillman had no choice but to call the police so he could get a court order to open the sealed casket.

As soon as it opened, Hoy knocked the policemen aside, grabbed May Alice by the shoulders, and shook her till her false eyelashes fell off.

"You stop it, May Alice! This ain't funny!"

Poor May Alice, it turned out, was really dead.

Nobody (except Hoy) objected to his arrest for disorderly conduct, striking a police officer, and interfering with a corpse. They were just glad May Alice's parents and Hoy's parents had already passed and weren't around to see what his so-called humor had led to.

As the police led Hoy away in handcuffs, May Alice's ghost floated out of the coffin and faded away. If anyone could have seen the spirit, they would have noted a demure, ladylike, and oh-so-satisfied smile on its ectoplasmic face.

THE END

The Baby Played Peek-A-Boo

by Ginny Fleming

Some people break down the Universal Ka with a blithe "Stuff Happens". I used to feel that way. Until the baby. . . . Now my philosophy is: "Stuff Happens When You Forget To Duck". One day, Big Sis and her hubby forgot to duck, and that's how I "inherited" my little nephew Zander.

He's a cute little diaper-loader, as knee-biters go. Looks a lot like his granddad — my dad — smells like him, too. All googly and squeeable, if one is susceptible to his ilk. Which, thank goodness, I'm not. But he comes in handy at the park. Let's just say, since Zander landed in my lap, I've become squeeable by association. Chicks dig me now.

Since Sis and Doofus took their big dirt-nap, I've been Zander's sole means of sustenance. I'm sorta like a momma penguin — though I draw the line at regurgitating into my famished nephew's mouth. I do, like a doting uncle, dangle that fish in the form of a padded spoon buzzing its way to a tasty landing in his gaping maw. Gad — the kid can put the Gerber away.

It was confusing and sad what happened to Sis and Stan the Doofus. Sad, because no little kid should be left behind when both parents bite the big one, and confusing because there wasn't a lot of evidence as to just what the hell happened.

All that was found at the scene was Zander in his highchair screaming to high heaven, baby food splattered everywhere (I'd seen the kid eat — this was normal) and a big smoldering hole in the wall where something had taken

Pair of Normal What?

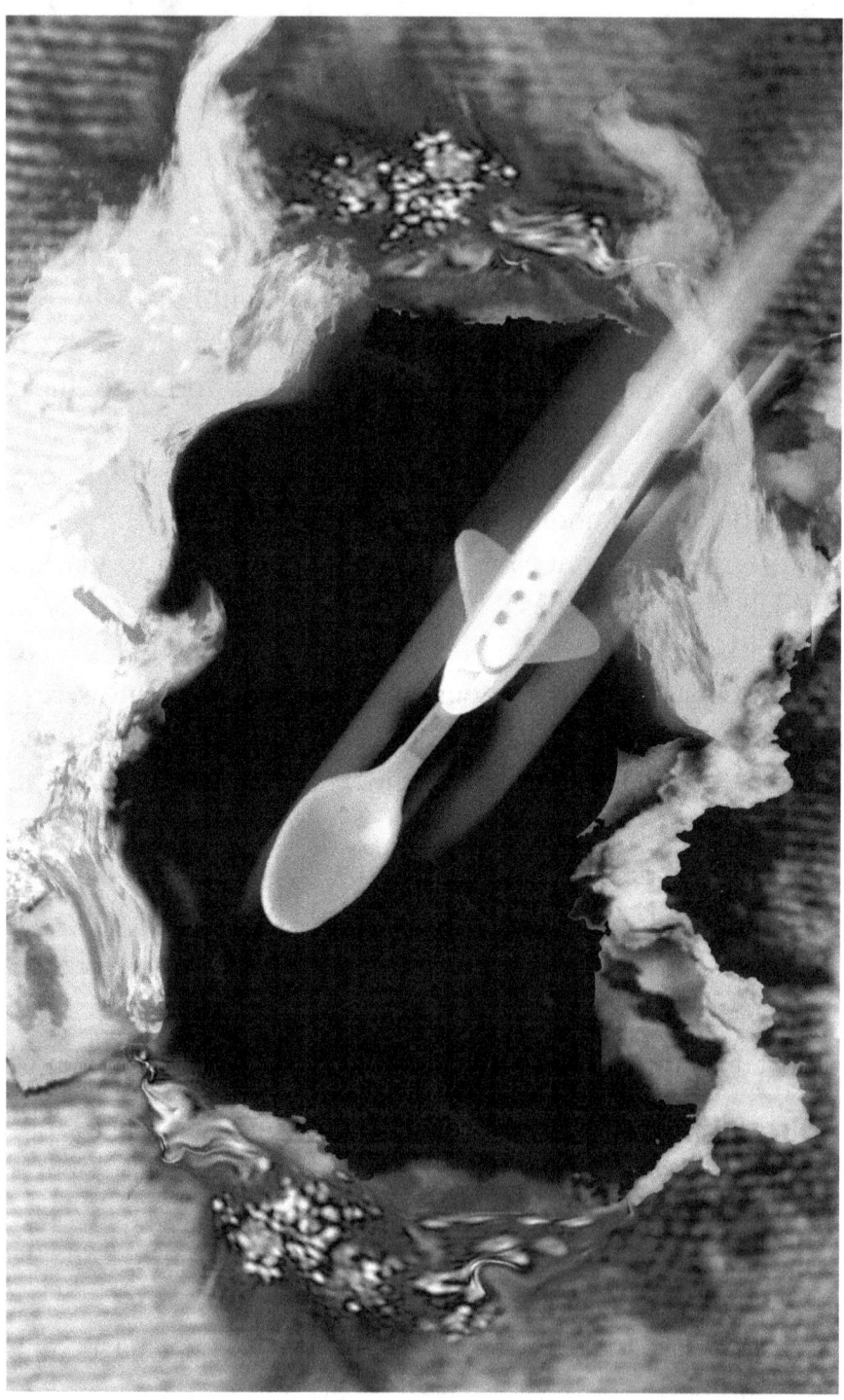

out Sis' prized credenza. Round and still smoking when I arrived — looked kinda like Marvin the Martian had finally met up with Bugs Bunny — lost his Martian cool and blasted the irritating, long-eared sumbitch to the moon. No trace of Sis and the big Doof except perhaps two tiny piles of ash — which CSI Toronto attributed to Sis' messy housecleaning, eh?

Toronto, in their wisdom, ruled abduction — Alien or Homegrown-Canadian. Perhaps, they said, the Doofus had angered the wrong guy, or Sis had defaulted down at "Honest Al's Cash For Gold". Anyhow, according to Toronto, this kind of thing happened all the time — and hey — here's your nephew, Big-Guy — we're outta here.

But I suspected it was far more than a case of "Pimp My Mess". Sis and the Doof were no more. They had ceased to be. They were dead, Jim — and they weren't ever coming back. But I also suspected what'd killed them.

Peek-A-Boo.

You see, just the week before, a scribbled letter came snail-mail from Sis. Basically, it said: "Skipper (Sis' childhood nickname for yours truly) — I need your help. WE need your help. You MUST come RIGHT NOW. No sleep since last Wednesday. Me and Stan are taking turns with Zander. He's getting stronger day by day. This is unreal — This is crazy — but for God's sake – if anything ever happ- (and here, the next few words appeared smeared . . . by tears?) never Peek-A-Boo. Do you understand? NEVER let little Zee pl— (another smear) —Boo. *It kills!!!*"

The word "kills" had been underlined to the point of tearing a small hole in the paper. The rest of the rambling letter was about mundane things. . . . No internet. Dog went missing the week before. Cat refuses to be in the same room with Zander. No food in the house, because neither one could leave the other alone with the baby. . . . I've held it back from the authorities, since I'd written it off as a bad case of the Post-Postpartum depression "crazies".

So, here we sit. Zander and his fav-boy uncle. We eat together, we bath together, we poop together — We be happy in our "Man-Cave". Mr. Mom ain't got nothing on me.

You might ask why the white cartoon "Mickey Mouse" gloves and soft restraints "chaining" him to the highchair? Well . . . Stuff happens. Or, more precisely, Peek-A-Boo happens.

And I, for one, want a little warning.

Ghost

by Dirk Grffin

my past surrounds
me falling
into now

what memory roots
my soul to the moment
spilling yesterdays into
tomorrow; i taper to
transparency

flash

dim
into insubstantial
breaths

A Moment in Mime

by Bonnie Abraham

It was a rushing-around, last-minute-shopping afternoon, just before Christmas. The mime in the city square attracted little attention, despite his obvious skill. At first his hands moved slowly, feeling the invisible barrier surrounding him, always exactly perpendicular to the ground, always evenly touching but never passing the "wall".

After a time, his movements became more hurried, then somewhat anxious as no opening appeared. The mime seemed frightened and short of breath; more and more rapidly, he searched for a way out, his hands always perpendicular, touching but never passing the invisible "box". A few people stopped and watched, but they stayed only briefly. Most only glanced as they hurried by.

The mime seemed to be suffocating, his movements jerky and erratic. He gasped for air and desperately mouthed, "Help me! Help me!" in silent screams.

His movements grew weaker, more frantic.

"Mommy!" cried a little girl from the now-gathering crowd, "He can't get out!" She wriggled free of her mother's restraining grasp. "We have to help him!" And she ran to the dying mime. She stopped just short of the "box" and held her hand palm out, parallel to his, touching his hand palm to palm.

Both figures froze for a moment in silent communication, then slowly, as though pushing against some tight membrane like a blown-up balloon, her little fingers curled inward between his until she held his hand. His face a mask of astonishment, the mime carefully felt for the "wall" with his free hand. It was gone! He took a deep breath of fresh air. "Thank you!" he cried as he hugged the little girl.

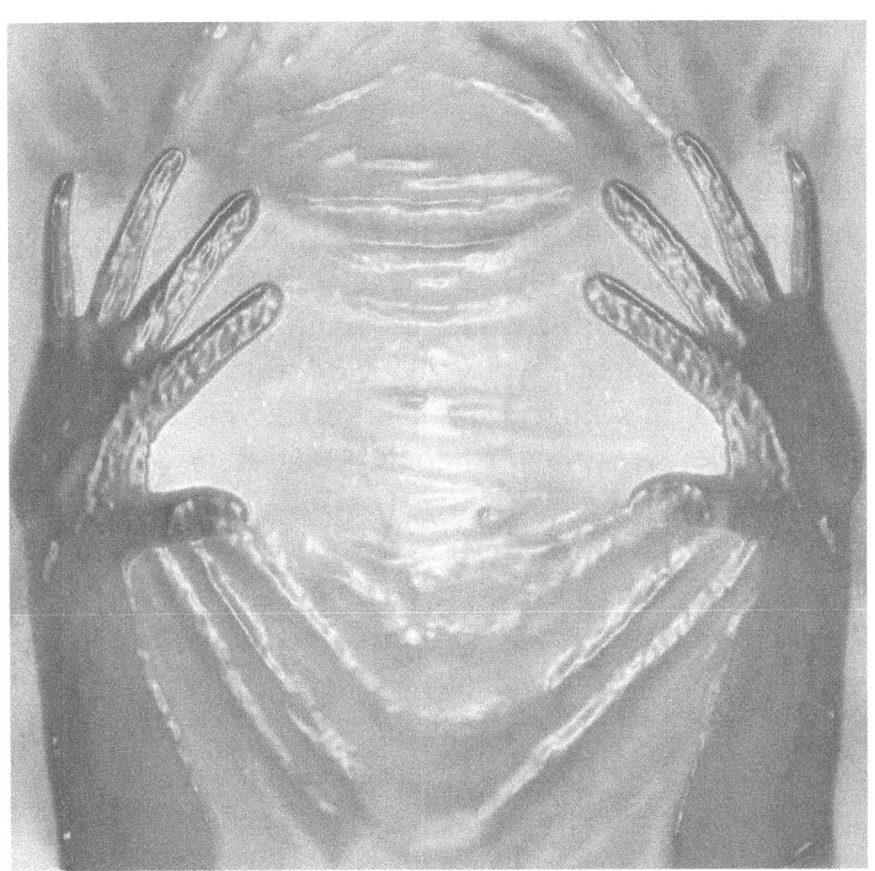

Demon Gun: Lock and Load

by Dirk D. Griffin

Joey Eliot was strictly small time. Even as a member of the Hellboyz with all their magically infused thugs and leaders, he was usually only allowed to carry a gun. The High Mages didn't think he was capable enough to handle the eldritch energies their schemes required. At 23, Joey was impatient with his prospects.

Tonight was going to change all that. Tonight, with the members of his old gang, all the preparations he'd made, the time spent secretly studying spells he'd finally get what the Hellboyz refused to give him: power. Real power. Power to take anything he wanted. The time for small spells was over; sure they were good for scamming a few bucks here and there, but tonight was going to be real magic.

Joey ran his fingers through his red, medium-length hair as he entered the abandoned Duke Beer warehouse in Royal Row's brewery district. Many businesses in this already depressed area were pushed over the economic edge by the Gravers' gang and the Hellboyz's ever-increasing demands for protection money. The arrival of crazed super-powered criminals and an alien invasion took care of the rest. Duke Beer had long ago packed up their toys and left for Mexico, cheaper labor and the immediate benefit of no super-criminals driving insurance rates through the roof.

Joey lugged his duffel bag full of mystical paraphernalia and other items necessary for tonight's summoning spell through the outer abandoned offices. He wiped the perspiration from his face and gave his hair a casual flip. The sweat didn't come from exertion; he was in excellent condition from hours in the gym sculpting his lean body while massaging his vanity. No, it was from pure anticipation.

Further in, he pulled out a torch, lit it, and moved through the inner offices leading to the main storage area where the floor plan opened up. Joey mounted the torch onto a column and dropped the duffel near the center of the cleared space. It had taken weeks, moving the litter of twisted and broken shelves, desks, cartons and file cabinets, but it was worth it. He placed more torches around the cleared floor filling the space with soft flickering shadows and light. He grabbed a dolly and walked it to a corner where some crumbled shelves were heaped and dug his way quickly through them, exposing the floor. He waved his hands, mumbled a few words, and a small stone floated from the floor to chest level revealing, instead of empty floor, the deactivated hulk of a Chief Designer, one of the main bosses in the Automaton Army.

The Automatons were an odd collection of robotic creatures that had attained sentience and arranged themselves in a hierarchy similar to mechanical engineers. The rumor went the first sentient Automaton is at the top of the heap and is responsible for creating all the later models. They were generally found robbing electronic and metal-works to create more of their kind, which they consider superior to all other life. Many believe the Automatons are waging an evolutionary war against anything not mechanical. Their soldiers range in size from larger bipedal forms as tall as 14 feet to smaller models less than a foot. There are, also, unproven rumors of the existence of nanite models. This Chief Designer model was gleaming steel with exposed areas burnished from the fires of battle. At approximately ten feet, it was an imposing figure of molded strength that, even dormant, seemed to radiate power.

Joey couldn't believe the luck he'd had seeing the heroes Acier and Mister Mento fly off after putting down the nest of damnable things infesting this warehouse. He had sorted through the mess for anything useful, and found this intact Designer unit; he first secured it with the concealment spell, then covered it with the debris from the room. This last bit eased his mind enough that he could leave it till after the local Super Sweepers clean-up crew came in to clear the shattered remains of the Automatons away.

He grabbed the stone from the air and pocketed it, then worked the dolly under the Chief unit and hauled it near the center of the room. Then, with a piece of chalk he drew two concentric circles, and a pentagram inside the smaller of the two. Finally, several glyphs and Latin phrases were copied painstakingly between the circles and throughout the inner circle and pentagram from a page that he had found torn from a copy of the Stygian Tome. Lastly, the Chief unit was placed in the middle of the whole effort and a mixture of salt, chalk and crushed bone poured over the outer circle of what would be the summoning portal. Joey was careful to leave an entry, a break in the powder on the circle, for them to come into it during the summoning. The whole process took the better part of the evening, but he had timed it well. Everything would be ready to begin by midnight. As he was placing torches at each point of the pentagram, his oldest friend, Levon arrived.

Levon Whit was dressed in his Hellboyz gang colors and bubbled with a nervous energy that Joey suspected was partly pharmaceutical. Joey and Whit grew up together in the shadow of the "Big I" The Infantino Medium Security Penitentiary for low to medium level paranormals in the old factory district. They were typical kids growing up in poverty under the hand of accidental parents and spent more time passing blame around for failure in their lives than doing anything about it. Misery and hard luck were family heirlooms their parents had inherited and dutifully passed on to the next generation. Joey and Levon were the children of petty thieves and confidence men and, as such, were taught to hate the establishment. "Take what you want, any way you can" was the motto of families like theirs and "do unto others before they do unto you" the golden rule. After all, the rationale went, the "rich've got more than they need anyway."

All his boyhood gang, the Dark Water Warriors, matriculated into Hellboyz U because of him. They'd spent their whole lives following Joey, but now, like him, they were all going nowhere. None of them even rated transformation spells to boost their basic abilities.

Sol Manderson arrived next. Always a little nervous, his small and wiry build amplified his quick movements. He seemed to twitch with excitement. Sol completed the Holy Trinity of the Dark Water Warriors. Joey, the leader, planning and giving orders, and Levon and Sol, his good Left and Right arms carrying out his commands. They always had each others' backs. It felt right again, being together. This meeting started to feel like a reunion and, in spite of the deadly serious business planned for the night, there was a party atmosphere as they prepared.

Pair of Normal What?

Jack Guarset and Bobby Barbarosa showed up together. They were an odd pair, but fiercely loyal to one another. Jack was cautious and thoughtful. Almost never flustered, he took few risks and when he did you could be sure he'd studied the matter for a bit. Bobby, on the other hand, was impulsive and jumped in with both feet before he'd ever seen the edge of the water. His temper was particularly volatile and he could flash hot, explode, go cool and turn on a smile all in an instant. Their trust was unquestioning and born from the camaraderie of fighting side by side.

Last in was Janet Crowe, a fiery brunette with an attractive athletic figure. She was five feet, five inches of pure high explosive energy. She was also Joey's girl. Lately, though she was mostly arm candy for a Hellboyz boss by the name of Puños de Fuego, who worked mostly out of Crown Heights. Puños de Fuego didn't know Janet was really playing him to help Joey get the things he needed. That was a secret known only by the Dark Water Warriors. She entered while the boys slapped each other on their backs and joked good-naturedly.

Joey dropped everything the second he saw her. They met midway, Janet jumping onto him and wrapping her legs around his waist. Joey caught her and they kissed passionately. "Good to see you, lover." she said, sliding down his body to stand next to him.

"You too, babe; you too. Did you get 'em?"

"What d'you think?" she cooed, and produced a small bag from the pocket of her tight jeans. Joey took the bag and opened it, pouring six rubies into his hand.

"Great. Just a little more to do, and we'll get this party started." He pulled a bone chalice and a Kris from the duffel bag. "Okay, everybody, you're going to need to donate a little blood. I'll show you how to do it, and don't worry; I've got a quick healing spell that'll fix you right up. He reached into the seemingly bottomless duffel and pulled out a white fleshy plant, then cut six thin pieces from it. "Now, watch me."

He held the Kris, blade down, over the cup clenching the blade with his other hand. He pulled the Kris quickly out of his fist, and blood flowed into the cup. He opened the bleeding appendage, palm up, slapped a piece of the plant over it, and mumbled a quick incantation. At once, the white plant turned deep red. Joey removed the plant and his hand was completely unharmed. He did this for each of the remaining members. After each had been bled and healed, he poured some wine into the chalice, swished it around to blend it before setting it aside.

"Hey, Joey," Bobby began, "how'd you score all this stuff?"

"This isn't even the best of it, man; it's easy to come by this kind of thing, if you have eyes in the right place." Joey cast a sidelong glance at Janet, who struck an innocent, who me? look at the group and everyone enjoyed a brief laugh.

"Levon, Solly." Joey said, still smiling from the easy laugh, "there's incense and a couple of burners in the bag, pull them out and get them ready. I copied off the chant and've been practicing it, but you've gotta join with me on some lines so that we can—" he paused to get the right phrase, "pool our spirits to summon as a group."

"What exactly are we summoning?" asked Jack, in slow tones tinged with concern.

"A demon. The binding should grant us all the power we need to get get us to the front of the line. Hell, we were here first, anyway." he spat out, boasting and complaining in the same breath. And he was right; the Dark Water Warriors did predate the Hellboyz, though they were never more than a turf gang protecting their neighborhood while pursuing petty theft and vandalism.

"What's the 'bot for?" Bobby Asked.

"That's the shell for the demon. It's gonna inhabit it, and with the glyphs I've painted on it, it'll be bound to that metal body." He snapped his fingers. "That reminds me." He reached to the bottom of the duffel and produced a large hat box. "I don't want to forget this." He opened the box and removed a large inhuman skull. It was big enough to fit over the head of the Chief Designer. Two great horns curved out from each side of the skull, then arced forward and down into a crescent shape. It was black as if it were burned.

"What the hell is that?" Janet shuddered slightly.

"Hell is exactly what it is, baby. This is a one hundred per cent pure demon skull. You can't believe what this thing cost me, and I don't mean cash." He stepped into the circle and placed the skull over the Chief's head, dipped his finger in the chalice of blood-wine and inscribed a glyph on the skull.

"I think we're ready to go. Each of you take your place on the points of the pentagram; use the entrance, here," he said indicating the open area where the powder hadn't been poured. He passed a ruby to each member of the circle, "Concentrate and don't forget when to speak and when to answer all together. Don't mess up the powder marking the outside of the circle: that's the most important thing. I don't think we wanna find out what happens if we screw this up."

Joey held his palm skyward with the ruby in it, chanted a short spell and the deep red stone floated up and began circling his head. He lit and took up the two incense burners swinging them in figure eights. He walked around the outside of the circle and began chanting."

"Noctis in umbris huius convenimus
Nocte ad profundum media clamavimus
ut tenebras divinas petamus"

He continued walking around the circle swinging the censers in varying patterns. The group answered his invocation with their own:

"Nocte ad profundum media clamavimus
ut tenebras divinas petamus"

Then in unison they quickened the pace:

"Sanguine apparete
igne apparete
inter haec ossa adeste"

And again the group intoned:

"Nocte ad profundum media clamavimus
ut tenebras divinas petamus"

The fire in the torches flared as the metal bones of the Chief Designer began to shift and change color. Joey entered the circle and laid the censures on either side of the Chief. Flesh began to rapidly grow over the robot; he completed the pouring of the powder closing the circle. The chant raised in pitch, their voices became louder; a shriek poured from the writhing creature of metal and flesh. As Joey continued the chant alone, he poured the chalice of blood-wine from head to toe onto the convulsing, screaming heap of crawling flesh and flashing steel:

"Per sanguinem!
Per ignem!"

Pajr of Normal What?

Again the torches flared as the warehouse echoed with what seemed the horrible shrieking of a thousand burning victims. The convulsing abomination erupted in fire, and bolted to its feet spinning and flinging fire into the corners of the room. As Hellboyz they were used to seeing all manner of abominations, but this was rapid and violent enough to startle them. Bobby and Janet dropped their crystals; Sol stumbled backwards and, in his rush, violated the circle. His foot slipped and swept through the powder wiping out a section of it. Jack fell to his knees and also damaged the circle. Levon, motionless, wet himself while rapidly mumbling Hail Marys over and over again. Joey made the worst mistake of all and fell into the burning tower of metal and flesh. He screamed briefly, and was gone in a burst of flame. The explosion threw everyone to the perimeter of the room and extinguished all the fires leaving it dark but for small patches of moonlight pouring in through the upper windows.

###

It was morning before anyone awoke. The first up was Sol. A direct beam of morning sunlight guttered through the upper windows and concentrated directly on his face. At first, he thought it was all a dream, but the smell of charred flesh mingled with burnt wood and metal convinced him of the reality. He immediately checked himself for damage even as he extricated himself from a tangle of shelves and boxes: "Joey? Levon? Bobby? Jack? Janet?" he shout-whispered repeatedly as he clawed along the floor afraid to stand up for reasons he couldn't articulate. He resembled a lizard crawling through the wreckage, looking first one way and then the next. Without noticing, he crossed into the circle and put his hand on it.

Pair of Normal What?

It was around twelve feet tall. He recognized the skull, though now it was crimson with black around the edges and the tips of the horns. The thick flesh was reptilian, with raised areas that seemed to be some kind of bone plating on the torso, arms and legs. There were great chains wrapped around the upper forearms and the gloves and boots were made of bone or metal. The whole of the creature was a blood red and midnight black. He then realized that the chest was moving up and down in slow, deep breaths.

Immediately, Sol backed away trying to make sense of the night before. Slowly he managed to gather the group and they compared notes. Each one was certain that they saw Joey destroyed by the demonic flames. Between all of them they managed a fairly accurate picture of the preceding evening's events. Finally, Janet barked in frustration, "Well, where does that leave us?" She looked at each man's face and then at the behemoth sprawled on the floor, "and that?"

Levon was the first to speak up. "Man, I don't know about the rest of you, but Joey was the only one I knew who had the whole picture. Did he share it with any of you?" The group looked guiltily at the floor and mumbled, each in their own way that Joey hadn't told them any more than the chant and to show up.

Jack suggested, "Well, wasn't part of the deal that the demon will do what we say?"

Levon stammered "Yeah. Yeah, that's right, we were all supposed to get some kind of power over that . . . thing, whatever it is." he finished in frustration.

Janet spoke again: "So, where are we on this?" The others stared in silence, first at her, then away from her. "Hell, let's just tell it to get up and serve us! Was there a special word or something buried in all that mumbo jumbo?"

Jack feebly offered, "Maybe we should just try n' wake it up?"

Sol erupted "Wake it up!" he bellowed. "Wake it up!" I don't even know if I wanna stick around, but you want to ask it out to breakfast?! What the hell are you thinking? We should just pack up our sorry asses and get the hell out of here before it wakes up! This thing was summoned from the deepest pit of hell and the guy who was supposed to know what he was doing is dead!" Waving his arms wildly, Sol began pacing and kicking various pieces of debris for emphasis while his voice began to resemble something between a shout and a wail. "You, Miss Janet. You want to know where we are? I'll tell you where we are: pants down, ass up SCREWED! Screwed with a capital S-C-R-E-W! And no Vaseline in sight. Look, I don't know 'bout the rest of you, but I'm hauling it out of here and if you've got any sense, you'll be right there with me." He paused to see if he was making any headway. The group sat there surrounded by the hellish mess of destruction, mouths agape, eyes wide, and pale as milk. Sol continued, "Guys? Hey, are you listening to me?"

A deep, baleful voice reverberated and rumbled, "Sit down, Sol." Hot brimstone-tinged air and enveloped him. Sol turned to see the creature, now standing — and looking taller than his original guess — its burning eyes seemed to bore into him. Sol felt very small and fragile as he sank first to his knees, then back on his haunches. Tiny squeaking sounds came from his mouth.

The creature continued to speak: "This wasn't the plan. I want you to know this. I don't know what went wrong, but I'm in here."

After a seeming stunned eternity, they asked collectively, "Joey?"

"Yes, Joey. I don't know what happened, I don't remember anything after I tripped."

"Y-You caught fire and exploded," shouted Levon. "You freakin' caught fire and exploded! That's what happened!"

"And now I'm in here, where the demon was supposed to be."

They all sat and considered the possibilities. They weren't used to reason, and as a result, became frustrated with trying to piece everything together. At last, Janet suggested: "Maybe you got the powers too? Can you do anything? Make anything? Throw fire? Something? That's what Puños de fuego does, he throws fire."

Joey considered his hands for a moment, and then held them out. They quickly let loose a burst of flames and in his hands appeared two guns, rough approximations of .45s, but scaled up for his size. They were more like LAW's with handles and triggers and sported dancing flames along the barrel. He raised one of the enormous weapons and fired it into a pile of debris causing it to erupt into flames. Then, as an afterthought, he waved his hand, and the fire went out.

Jack let out a long slow whistle and said, "Now that's cool." There was general agreement among them that cool pretty much covered it.

"If I think about it, I seem to know what I can do. Ideas are coming to me." Without warning he produced a flame in one hand and tossed it at Levon's feet. The flame disappeared as quickly as it had appeared after it engulfed

Levon. It changed him, he seemed tougher, more muscular, and instead of Hellboyz clothes, he was wearing a leather suit similar to Joey's new appearance. He also held a matching pair of .45s, flames and all. It took a few seconds, but Levon managed to exhale a quiet, excited, "Wicked! Dude. This is so wicked!"

"Janet," Joey began, "you wanted to know where this left us. I'll tell you where: powerful enough to do exactly what we wanted. We're taking this town from the Hellboyz first. Then, were gonna take anything else we want. If anyone is dumb enough to get in our way. . . ," he fired a quick burst of hellfire from his guns obliterating an overturned desk and some chairs, "we'll let these bad boys deal with them." He looked at his friends, he could see their enhanced hell-forms in his mind; he knew what each would become in his altering flames, and realized that they were powerful enough to take what they wanted. "From now on," he proclaimed, "this is Demon Gun Territory!"

The Jesus of Another Time and Dimension.

by J. Baumgartle

He's met someone.
In sitting on the edge of the bed
it comes to me, as normal a thought
as if I had read it in the paper.
—Time does move on.
People tire of always being "set apart,"
of keeping in mind "the big picture."

They walk side by side in my mind,
listening, being, not an ideal
but themselves.
There is peace in rapport,
an understood verb
in the fragments of conversation.

Here, there are no rules.
Here, there is time to discover
identity in another person's eyes,
to accept, adapt, in the safety of love.

Families, he will discover, aren't perfect.
He will probably, at some time,
be embarrassed by his children's behavior;
be totally enamored of their potential;
find himself going bald. . . .
Try to draw close a woman
going through menopause;
have to juggle livelihood
with personal time and passions;
learn not to expect, just to live.

And then.
And then laugh as it all slips through his fingers.

Fall Bounty

by Janet Wolanin Alexander

The afternoon was cool, but pleasant — the wind intermittent, the sky clear, and the sun shining. My horse Highlander and I were patrolling the state forest for litter. Along the ridge, yellow leaves rained upon us like manna from heaven, and rainwater sparkled like diamonds in the curled leaves mulching the trail.

At the bottom of a long, steep descent, we found ourselves coming up behind two hikers. Before we got within talking distance, they turned left onto a hiking trail. Highlander and I continued along the multi-use one.

As soon as we crossed a dry stream bed, I spotted a Styrofoam "peanut" hanging from a signless stake of rebar on the left. I plucked the tidbit off and was placing it in my Kroger bag when a Voice pronounced, "That's mine."

I looked over my shoulder expecting to see the hikers. But neither was there.

The Voice repeated, "That's mine." On second thought, perhaps it had come from On High.

Wondering "WHAT was His — the manna or the diamonds," I looked up and saw God way up in a deer stand manifesting as a hunter in full camouflage.

He added, "Doe urine."

Not at all comprehending His message, I eloquently replied, "Huh?"

He repeated, "Doe urine."

Still not understanding this totally unanticipated, divine message, I again mumbled, "Huh?"

"That thing you just picked up — it's doe urine and you can just toss it under this tree."

Fumbling to retrieve the packing chip from my bag, I collected myself enough to string together a few words. "I'm picking up litter," I stammered.

As we moved on, He blessed us with a grateful "thank you." I was so relieved to hear I had earned His approval! A few twists and turns down the trail, a third form of prosperity appeared – a quarter moon hanging in the sky next to the round, slowly setting sun.

Manna, diamonds, coins, and a message from Above — not a bad haul for one day!

NOTE: Sadly, the lovely horse trail that provided the setting for this true story on November 7, 2008, the Mountain Grove Trail of the Clark State Forest in Southern Indiana, was destroyed by an EF4 tornado on March 2, 2012.

Messenger

by Samantha Lopez

I read your obituary again
Walls close in around me until I can't breathe
I run to decorative spires
I rage against the black-robed, collared surrogate for God
Who can do nothing to ease my pain
In glimpses, I see my angel watch over me
A guide assigned to stay by my side
A feather touch from which I turn

I exit a club where I seek solace,
Bright lights and loud drums attempt to distract from the missing piece of my heart
Pain and love war inside me, finally culminating in
The release of tears which echo across the lake nearby
I fall to my knees at the edge. Gentle waves lap upon the shore
In the water's reflection, my angel appears again, white glow shimmers,
Delivers the message she's been trying to give:
Peace. For in love, you are still with me.

Messing With Mother Nature

by T. Lee Harris

The battered skimmer shot through a gap in the trees that looked too small for a vehicle to negotiate and bounced over the uneven surface of the clearing beyond. Devlyn Frost gripped the controls and aimed for the treeless horizon. "Finally out of the forest," he said through gritted teeth. "Are they still back there?"

RSS 104 squirmed against his shoulder harness for a better view. "I'll check, but how I'm supposed to detect a buncha walking trees in the middle of a buncha *other* trees—" A volley of thorn-like projectiles clattered against the window. Russ swiveled around and slid farther down in his seat. "Yeah. They're back there."

Dev slid an amused glance at his android companion.

"Hey!" Russ said. "My embedded personality came from a computer systems developer. There is nothing in that profile to make me cool with being torn apart by a lynch mob of technophobic sentient plants."

No more than there is in the background of a former Atlanta-plex file clerk, Frost mused. "Point taken," he said aloud. "Hold on, we got rocky outcroppings ahead. That might mean we're far enough from the Gaean interference to regain a satellite lock. I want map function back, then we get the hell outta here."

Russ craned back again, watching the lush forest recede. In the not-distant-enough distance, figures emerged, looking like the trees had split off smaller, mobile versions of themselves. The Gaeans moved swiftly across the scrubby ground in an odd, graceful gait as if they were ice-skating on dry land.

"*Holy crap!* The tree-dudes just left the Eden. Man! Who'da thought taking a few cuttings and samples would rile them up so bad?"

Dev shoved the controls forward. The old rattletrap wasn't built for that kind of strain and her boosters screamed, but the gap between them and their pursuers widened. "Maybe the researcher who paid us beaucoup credits to get those cuttings and samples?"

"Mmmmm. Good guess," Russ said, settling back into his seat. He regretted the move. Instead of ambulatory trees chasing them, he now had a full-screen view of a towering wall of rock getting closer by the second. "Uhhhhhh, Chief. . . ?"

Up close, the outcropping looked like a row of jagged teeth. Devlyn slotted the skimmer through a crumbled section only to find the ground beneath them dropped away on the other side. Fighting panic, he fumbled with the console. Convincing the craft to switch from mag-lift to short-term glider mode — never an easy feat — was made more difficult by the fact his fingers suddenly seemed to belong to someone else. Finally, the engines shuddered. The plunging skimmer leveled out and Dev brought it in for a relatively smooth landing on the arroyo floor.

"Good thing I don't have bodily functions, or we'd be replacing this seat," Russ said.

"We made it, didn't we?"

"Ooooh, lissen to Mr. Cool! You were swearing the whole time."

"I was?" Frost tried to release his death-grip on the controls.

"Yeah. It was great!" Glancing at the top of the rock wall, the android added, "Think we lost 'em?"

Dev forced his fingers to uncurl. "Doubt it. If they were pissed enough to leave their forest, they won't let a little thing like a thirty-foot drop stop them." He eyed the sky. "They might think twice about an electrical storm headed this way, though."

"Electrical storm?" Russ followed his partner's gaze. The sky to the west was slate gray and a line of towering, black clouds stretched across the horizon, moving toward them at a fast clip. From time to time, lightning flashed, momentarily painting the underside of the front brilliant blue-white. "Oooooh. *That* storm. That's ugly."

"Not much hope of satellite contact until it passes, either," Devlyn said. He looked around. "We're too visible here. Our happy plant-buddies will spot us as soon as they top that rise."

He pointed the vehicle toward higher ground and maneuvered so it was obscured by several large boulders and piles of rockfall. They added to the impromptu camouflage with dried brush and tumbleweeds. Skimmer well-concealed, Russ turned his attention to the approaching storm. "That's movin' pretty fast. It'll probably be right over us in thirty — mebbe forty minutes. What do you wanna do, Chief?"

Devlyn didn't answer. He was leaning back, using the curve of a boulder as support, scanning the cliff face.

"Chief?"

"I hate it when you call me that," Frost said without looking away from the escarpment. "Help me get the gear out of the skimmer. I have an idea. Leave the big stuff, just our packs, the weapons and the sample boxes for now."

Pajr of Normal What?

The dual threat of fast-moving storm and angry Gaeans was an effective spur, they unpacked the skimmer in record time. Devlyn was securing his backpack when Russ reached past him for the tent. "Oh, leave that. I feel like I'm inside a pumpkin in that damned thing. Whatever possessed you to buy an orange pop-up shelter, anyway?"

"You *told* me to buy the cheapest I could find."

"I *said* 'find the best deal'. Your logic circuits are fried."

Russ ignored him. "Okay, no tent. Where do we ride out the storm?"

Dev grinned and pointed to a dark smudge half-way up the precipice. "Cave."

They'd expected a hard climb, but barely-visible handholds that Frost had noticed from the ground soon gave way to a steep stair-like path that led directly to a projecting ledge framed by the narrow arch of a cave's mouth.

"This is amazing. It's not a natural cavern at all," Devlyn said, stepping in and holding the sol-torch high. His voice echoed off the artificially smooth walls and seemed to vanish into the shadows at the back. "Y'know what? I think this is an old outpost from the Wars."

"That would sure explain why it's on the edge of a major Nova Terra Eden," the android said.

Dev was silent. The Wars had ended over a hundred years before, but reminders of them were everywhere. The news footage and vids they'd shown in his secondary school global history class had given him nightmares for months.

The Gaea Wars; named for the bio-engineer turned eco-terrorist who triggered them in the middle of the last century. Angered by the indifference of government and big corporations to Global Warming, genetic modification, pollution and the other indignities the Earth suffered, Gail Honigbaum had spearheaded a movement to become one with the natural world. Turning her back on humanity, Gail Honigbaum took the name Gaea after the primal Greek goddess of the Earth. She called her movement Nova Terra. Using science, she altered herself and her followers until they became more plant or insect than human. She then unleashed her anger in the form of a mutagen that caused native fauna to grow at a prodigious rate, starting with the desolate strip mines in the mountains of West Virginia, turning them into verdant, apparent paradises in a matter of weeks. She called them her Edens. The catch was that these Edens were decidedly hostile to Adam and Eve. As the wildernesses spread globally, humanity found itself at war with armies of insectoid and plant-like creatures. They swarmed population centers, bringing destruction in their wake. Residents of the combat zones were killed or absorbed into the ranks of drone soldiers. Cities, roads and factories crumbled and disappeared under fast-growing primal forests.

With society on the brink of collapse, humanity fought back. It was a long and hard fight that left the world forever changed in its wake.

"Chie — Dev? You okay?"

Shaking off history, Devlyn said, "Yeah. Just fine."

"Y'didn't look fine. Y'looked kinda . . . I dunno . . . Not there."

"I'm *fine*." Abruptly snagging a rifle and a pair of binoculars, Frost strode back to the entrance. "With this elevation we ought to have a great view — *crapola!* Those things move fast. They're already below us."

Russ grabbed another set of glasses, but froze in mid-move; his synth-skin crawled with the feeling of being watched. Pivoting slowly, he discovered a man in uniform standing motionless in the shadows at the back of the chamber. "Uuuuhhhh, Chief? We got company."

"Huh?" Devlyn lowered the binoculars, but before he turned, the figure winked out.

Russ took a step back. "Whoooa, I didn't know I had a Creeped Out circuit, but it's in overdrive now."

"What are you talking about?"

"The ghost!" The android pointed into the now-vacant shadows. "Right there!"

"There's no such thing as ghosts," Dev said dismissively.

"Yeah? What just flittered away, then?"

"The electrical storm must be messing with your sensors. Flittered. Is that even a word?" He returned to his surveillance. The light outside had turned an eerie green due to the approaching storm. "Well, the good news is that they haven't spotted the skimmer. The bad news is they haven't given up or moved on."

"Uh huh." Russ said, slowly approaching the place the apparition had stood. It *looked* empty. It *scanned* empty. Experimentally, he waved a hand though the empty air. Not even a temperature variation.

"Hey," Frost said, turning slightly. "Your glitch reminded me, we didn't check if there were any back doors to this place. If I remember correctly, some of these wartime boltholes had built-in escape hatches."

When Russ didn't respond, Dev turned around and called, "Hey! Tin Man! Did you rust back there?"

"Hunh?" The android looked up. "Yeah . . . well . . . guess I'll just go check if there's a back door . . . or somethin'."

The sol-torch cut through the shadows, revealing two doorways near the back of the main room. Russ poked his head into the first and found himself in what must have been the barracks. Eight bunk niches were cut into the solid rock, but the bedding they'd once contained was long gone. The barren niches reminded him uncomfortably of photos he'd seen of ancient catacombs. Making sure the only door from there led to what had been a shower and bathroom area, he ducked back out.

The second door led to a room with several ruined tables and chairs. An alcove off this one contained the remains of cooking equipment. Labeling this one as the mess hall seemed to be a safe bet. A single door at the far end of the mess hall led to a room filled with banks of deteriorating equipment. Curiosity overcame apprehension as Russ poked through the remains trying to figure out what its function might have been. He was lifting a broken circuit board that he thought might have been part of a spectral analyzer, when he felt a familiar, but uncomfortable sensation. Slowly lowering the board, he turned. The uniformed man was there again.

"Hey, man, hi," Russ said carefully setting the circuit board down. "Not doin' anything. Really! Just lookin' around."

The figure winked out again.

Russ bolted through the mess hall and skidded to a halt back in the main chamber.

Devlyn looked away from the field glasses. "Did you find anything back there?"

"Uuuuuh, no. Just a few rooms, some busted equipment and trashed furniture." He went over to stand beside his human partner. "They still down there?"

"Yeah. They seem real hesitant to leave that clearing. They start up the ravine, get to the top of that rockfall over there, then rush back."

"Weird."

The storm filled the western sky now. Outside, the wind picked up, spawning dust devils along the floor of the arroyo and stirring the dry brush covering the skimmer. The Gaeans continued to mill around in the area just below the mouth of the cave — too close to the vehicle for Devlyn's comfort. "Come on, you walking broccoli, what are you hanging around for? Nothing to see here, move along."

Thunder rumbled in the distance. Dev said, "Wow. That got a reaction. They kind of jumped."

"Yeah? I've heard stories that the tree guys have a thing about lightning. Wonder if it might be true."

"It'd be great if it was. You can kind of see why. Trees and lightning don't exactly play well together."

As if on cue, lightning strobed within the fast-moving cloud bank. The creatures below looked up sharply. A bolt struck near the mouth of the cave, exploding against the canyon wall with a deafening crash. Devlyn and Russ dived and rolled aside.

"Wow," Frost said, wiggling a finger in his ear to clear the ringing. "That was a close hit. You okay over there?"

Russ had dived well back into the cavern. He sat up and assessed himself. "I think so. Nothing seems to be fried, anyway."

"Good." Devlyn was on the move again, back to his observation post. He raised the field glasses. "Wait! They're gone," he muttered scanning the ground below. "Where the hell are they? I thought I wanted them gone, but. . . ." He caught movement toward the jagged rock wall. Sweeping the binoculars toward the movement, he whooped, "All right! Run you bastard vegetables! Looks like the stories were right, Russ."

Lightning cracked again, farther away and the hunters hastened their odd, skating run to vanish through the crevasse and into the darkness beyond.

"Yes! Score one for the fury of Mother Nature." He lowered the binoculars, his face exultant. "There's something ironic there."

Russ grinned, too, but the grin faded as the ghost reappeared right behind Devlyn. The translucent man turned toward him and gave him an unmistakable thumbs up, then vanished.

Unaware, Dev stretched and stifled a yawn. "Okay, the adrenaline rush just shut off. I'm going to grab the bedroll and catch some Zs."

Russ sidled over and looked hard where the apparition had stood. "Ummm yeah." He settled down, back against the wall. "You do that. I don't need shutdown for another couple days, yet. I'll stay here — just in case."

The storm raged through the night, but dawn brought blue skies and a clear satellite connection.

Morning light also confirmed something felt, but not really seen, in the rush to get up and away from their pursuers: the handholds closer to the ground weren't as well-defined as the ones farther up. It was probably a safety precaution against Gaeans climbing up to the outpost themselves, but regardless of original intent, it would make getting their equipment down more difficult. Instead, they rigged a pulley so Russ could lower the gear to where Frost waited beside the idling skimmer.

Pajr of Normal What?

The storm was gone, but wind still whistled through the arroyo, kicking up dust devils and making the lowered bundles twist and swing. It all went well until the last load, the three cryo cases containing the collected Gaean samples that had started all the hoohah. They were almost in Devlyn's outstretched arms when a particularly strong gust of wind snagged the netted load, swinging it away and banging it against the rockface. Russ, unprepared for the impact, lost his hold on the line. The cases went into freefall.

He didn't dare watch. From below came much crashing, swearing and pinging of falling stones — then silence.

After a moment, Russ called, "Did you catch it? Pleeeease tell me you caught it."

"Damn straight I did," Devlyn shouted back. "This crap nearly got us killed. I want to get *paid* for it."

Relieved, Russ leaned out to see his partner gently lowering the net bag to the ground. "That's good, 'cause I sure as hell don't wanna go back and—" The hand he'd placed against the cave's mouth to steady himself touched the singe that marked the site of the lighting strike. Electricity arced and he was suddenly lying several feet away, staring at the smooth ceiling of the room.

"Whooooa!" he groaned, sitting up woozily just as Devlyn scrambled up into the cavern, pistol drawn, rifle slung over his back.

"What happened?" Frost demanded.

"Not sure. I leaned against the rock right there and POW! I took a helluva jolt."

Holstering the pistol, Frost cautiously examined the wall and was amazed to see glints of metal through the lightning scorch. The stronger daylight also showed the previous evening's strike hadn't been the first to hit that spot. Tilting his head, he followed the carbon streaks down a ways, then said, "Hey! Take a look at this! I think there's some kind of conduit embedded here."

There was and it still hummed with power. Now that he was looking for it, Russ easily traced the conduit down the cliff and to the rockfall just up the canyon.

Devlyn climbed over the rockpile. "No wonder the killer weeds didn't want to go over this rise. There's a grid inset into the ground over here. Looks like a collection and dispersal unit."

"Sure does," Russ said, peering around his partner. "I'm betting if we follow the other close strikes from last night, we'll find more of these and circuits leading from them into the outpost. But why?"

Dev crouched thoughtfully beside their find, then said, "I might know why." He straightened and looked up toward their former shelter. "Toward the end of the wars, the human factions were experimenting with ways to contain or repel the Gaean forces. If I remember correctly, some of those experiments involved harnessing natural forms of energy for the purpose."

"So this is a kind of gigantic electric fence?"

"Looks more like a humongous bug zapper to me."

"Bug zapper." Russ looked around and nodded. "I can dig it."

"Anyway, it did a damn good job last night. I don't want to think what could have happened if those Gaeans had found the skimmer — or us." Turning away, he dusted off his hands and headed back toward the vehicle. "C'mon. Let's get this show on the road!"

Sliding into the pilot's seat, Dev resumed punching buttons. "Aaannnnd we want thattaway!" he said, locking in the co-ordinates. "Couple days and we'll be back at ABQ-plex to collect the rest of our fee."

Russ stowed the last of the gear and secured the hatch. Looking up toward the cave mouth and the shimmering figure just visible beside it, he gave a thumbs up, then climbed into the skimmer. "Hit it, Chief!"

Fangs For Nothing

by Marian Allen

I am sitting around, doing nothing in the world except mind my own business, which is namely The Retro Fit, a nostalgia shop in Ithaca, New York. I am bitten by a vampire in 1935, so I save on overhead by selling my own stuff as I tire of it. And, no, I do not sparkle, I am sorry to say. Sparkling used to be a handicap to vampires turned by elders with the sparkle gene; but ever since TWILIGHT, sparklers who go out in the sunlight have to beat blood donors off with sticks.

As I say, I am taking it easy this day I am talking about, sitting in my apartment above the shop with my feet up, sipping coffee from a mug which says Keep Calm and Drink Blood, when the telephone rings.

In case you are too young to know, "telephone" is what we used to call a land line, back when phones were too big to fit in your pocket and had to be connected to the wall all the time by a wire. I have a cell phone, of course, but many of Us do not stay current with the times, and I keep a land line as a courtesy to my many friends and acquaintances who are such old-fashioned folk as this.

When the telephone rings, I expect it to be a telemarketer or some irritating personage such as this. I understand they often interrupt regular people during dinner, so I consider it one of my charities to keep them talking as long as possible, as they do not interrupt me during *my* dinner, unless I happen to track one of them down, in which case I interrupt them during my dinner.

However, as it happens, this is not a telemarketer calling me on my old-fashioned land line telephone, it is nobody else but Vlad the Roumanian, the person who has a permanent place in the number one spot on my "do not want to hear from" list.

Do not get me wrong. I have nothing but good to say about Vlad the Roumanian. In fact, I never hear anyone say anything but good about Vlad the Roumanian. Not more than once, anyway.

"Is this Miss Garnet Satin?"

I confirm that it is. If I can deny it and get away with it, I will. Usually, if Vlad the Roumanian wants something, he will have one of his guys relay the message. If it is personal, he will visit in person. If he calls on the telephone, it is usually that somebody he thinks well of asks him a favor, and he is passing it on. This way, the person who asks the favor cannot say Vlad the Roumanian does not try to grant it, and Vlad the Roumanian has somebody to punish if the favor-granting attempt should fail.

"Miss Garnet Satin, I have a favor to ask of you. It is actually a friend of mine who asks this favor, but I will be most pleased if you will do this small thing for him."

I am not a rocket scientist, but I know better than to appear less than enthusiastic, so I assure Vlad the Roumanian that I will like nothing better than to do whatever he and his friend want or need.

"This is very thoughtful of you, Miss Garnet Satin," says Vlad the Roumanian. "This thing my friend needs you to do is a very small thing, indeed. You hear me speak of my friend Mansfield Parker, now and again?"

Now, it is not necessarily smart or healthy to remember what Vlad the Roumanian speaks of, so I say, "I do not know. Do I?"

Vlad the Roumanian makes a dry, scratchy sound that serves him as a laugh. "It will make things easier if you do."

"Then I do."

"This friend of mine lives in a large brown house of the Craftsman style on Catalpa Street. You help him find a guy to put up a cast-iron fence around his yard when he moves in not long ago."

By "not long ago," Vlad the Roumanian means a quarter of a century ago, but time is like this for those of Us who live to ripe old ages.

"I sincerely hope the fence continues to give satisfaction," I say.

"I hear no complaints," says Vlad the Roumanian, which relieves me more than somewhat. "This matter is another matter, entirely. Mr. Mansfield Parker," he says, "is the kind of a bird who sleeps in a coffin during the day. Somebody turns him into one of Us on the very night Mr. Mansfield Parker goes to see the first release of the original Nosferatu, and he never gets over it."

"My, my," I say, as noncommittally as possible.

"Mr. Mansfield Parker also never gets over the idea that swarms of regular people are prowling around and about, intent on breaking into his coffin and exposing him to the sunlight."

Now, direct sunlight is no better for vampires than it is for anybody else, but most of us can tolerate a reasonable amount. I doubt a sudden burst of daylight will do more than give this Mansfield Parker a sneezing fit, but this, I do not say. I also do not say that, if he is so terrified of regular people, he needs to get a bodyguard, and the reason I do not say this is that I am afraid Vlad the Roumanian will think I am volunteering for the job which, to be perfectly honest, I am not.

"You will be thinking that what my friend needs is a Magyar." Magyar is our word for regular people who, for various and sundry reasons, guard us with their lives. "As a matter of fact, my friend has one of these. But my friend is beginning to doubt his Magyar's total devotion. My friend suspects his Magyar of being no Magyar at all, but just a guy in it for the cabbage. My friend suspects his maybe-not-a-Magyar is deserting him while he sleeps, leaving him vulnerable to attack by mobs of hysterical peasants armed with torches and pitchforks."

I try to imagine the citizens of Ithaca, New York, as such a mob, and fail.

"What I wish for you to do," says Vlad the Roumanian, "is investigate the situation."

I open my mouth to protest that I am a simple businesswoman, not an investigator, but my brain gets a stranglehold on my tongue and shows it what Vlad the Roumanian will do to my neck if I contradict him, and I simply make a compliant noise into the telephone.

The next day I go to Catalpa Street and put the house under observation. Of course, if the Magyar does not leave by the front door, I will not assume he does not leave at all. You know what Vlad the Roumanian says about assumptions: "Never assume. It makes you disappear without a trace."

Sure enough, though, the front door opens, and who should come out but Jasper Caufmann. Jasper Caufmann is the regular guy I work with the last time Vlad the Roumanian pays me the doubtful compliment of asking me to investigate something for him. Why, I wonder, does Vlad the Roumanian not tell me that Mansfield Parker's Maygar is my old acquaintance? Does he think I will take my life in my hands and turn down the assignment, if I know this? Or does he simply not consider it important, one regular guy being pretty much the same as another in Vlad the Roumanian's eyes?

At any rate, this is none other than Jasper Caufman, so plump and pale he could play the part of a guy drowned two days ago and not need much makeup whatsoever.

I slip up behind him as he fumbles with his car keys and say, "Boo."

Caufmann jerks so hard, his keys fly up into the air and land, with a merry jingle, on his nearly bald head. His eyes cross, and I think he may collapse in a piddle of nerves, but this he does not do.

We go back inside, and he speaks to me, saying as follows: "I cannot stay here. I know I take an oath, and I take the money every week, and I begin well. I stay here all day every day for three months. Then I start having weird feelings. I feel that I am not alone in the house. There is something creepy here."

"Besides you?"

"Besides my employer."

Now that he mentions it, I feel something, too.

"Please do not report me to my employer. Or, worse yet, to your employer. Please, Garnet — Miss Satin!" His fingers curl as if he is about to grasp me by something. As I can think of nothing by which I wish to be grasped by this particular guy, I hold up a hand in a cease-and-desist manner.

"I promise," I say. Naturally, this is a lie. I do not feel guilty for telling this lie because, if he is not such a chump,

Jasper Caufmann will know I am not so foolish as to keep anything from Vlad the Roumanian.

Jasper relaxes somewhat after this, although he still fidgets and cracks his knuckles and wipes his moist brow with a cheap pocket handkerchief.

I, myself, sense a spirit of menace in the house. If I am not already dead, I will be worrying that I may become that way.

This seems like a good time to do some of this investigating which Vlad the Roumanian has tasked me to do, so I ask, "When does this creepy feeling begin? How long ago?"

"Three days ago. The first day, I stick it out. When Mr. Parker gets up after sunset, I ask him if he is angry about something. He says he is not. I tell him about the feeling, and he seems pleased, thinking I am afraid of him."

"You are not?"

Jasper pulls down the collar of his shirt, exposing a crucifix on a chain around his neck. He looks at me expectantly, so I cringe and hiss. Anything which indicates that I prefer him to maintain all possible distance is something which I wish to encourage.

"What brings this feeling on? Do you feel it every day? From the time you enter the house until you leave, or from the time your employer retires until the time he rises?"

"From shortly after he retires until shortly before he rejoins me here and tells me I am dismissed."

"Do you feel it outside, during the time you abandon your employer and run away?"

Jasper draws himself up with what dignity he can manage and says, "I do not run away. I drive down the street and keep watch from the coffee shop, from which I can clearly see the front door."

"This," I say, "will be a big help, if anyone intent on attacking your employer walks up to the front door and takes enough time attacking for you to drive back and stop them. Assuming, of course, you do not drive the other way by mistake."

He gives me a sorrowful look, such as is meant to reproach me for my unkindness, but death means never having to say you are sorry.

"What do you do differently on the day this feeling first hits?"

"Nothing."

"What do you do differently on the day this feeling first hits?"

"Nothing, I tell you."

"What do you do diff—"

"Nothing!"

His heart pounds. My fangs descend from my upper gums, but not even bloodlust can induce me to bite the sweaty neck in the chair across from mine.

It is time, I decide, to use the power of vampire glamour on him. This, in case you do not know, is the ability to influence the weak-minded to bend them to your will. It is a very useful ability to have, and it has the additional benefit of being spelled funny, unless you happen to be British, in which case you spell it glamor, which is funny in Britain.

So I glamour him.

Jasper's face loosens and his eyes glaze over. Of course, his pulse also slows, and my automatic hunger simmers down.

Still, I am never one to waste a good thing, and I realize Jasper, being in my power, will now not be able to evade my question. Of course, he will not be able to answer it either, as he is so slack-jawed he is almost drooling.

"Show me what you do differently the first time you feel the creepy feeling here," I say.

Jasper stands. I follow him into the kitchen. He goes into the walk-in pantry, which is stocked with tins of sardines, cans of soup, bottled water, crackers, and other dull fare such as a guy who has consumed nothing but fresh blood since 1922 might suppose regular guys eat.

Jasper picks up a tin of sardines and pulls off the key affixed to its underside. As he does so, he cries out and sticks his finger in his mouth. He pulls his finger out, scowls at it, makes a face, and kicks petulantly at the edge of the shelving unit. The unit swings open, revealing what appears to be a shrine. He staggers backward as if struck by something physical.

I understand, as the creepy feeling is much stronger with the shrine in view. Nevertheless, when Jasper Caufmann continues his reenactment by dropping his food and bolting out of the house, slamming the front door behind him, I step forward and look at what has been revealed.

There is a shelf built between the studs behind the shelving unit. The niche thus created is lined with cloth which is probably once white, shot through with gold thread, although not much besides the metallic part is now left. Pocket mirrors are propped up in the back and at the sides, reflecting a small yellow glazed clay figure with four legs, a tail, and pointed ears. It is standing up on its hind legs and playing a kazoo. I reach out to pick up the figure and look at it more closely, but the closer my hand gets to it, the more I feel endangered. My hand will not get near the little figure. My fingers will not close around it.

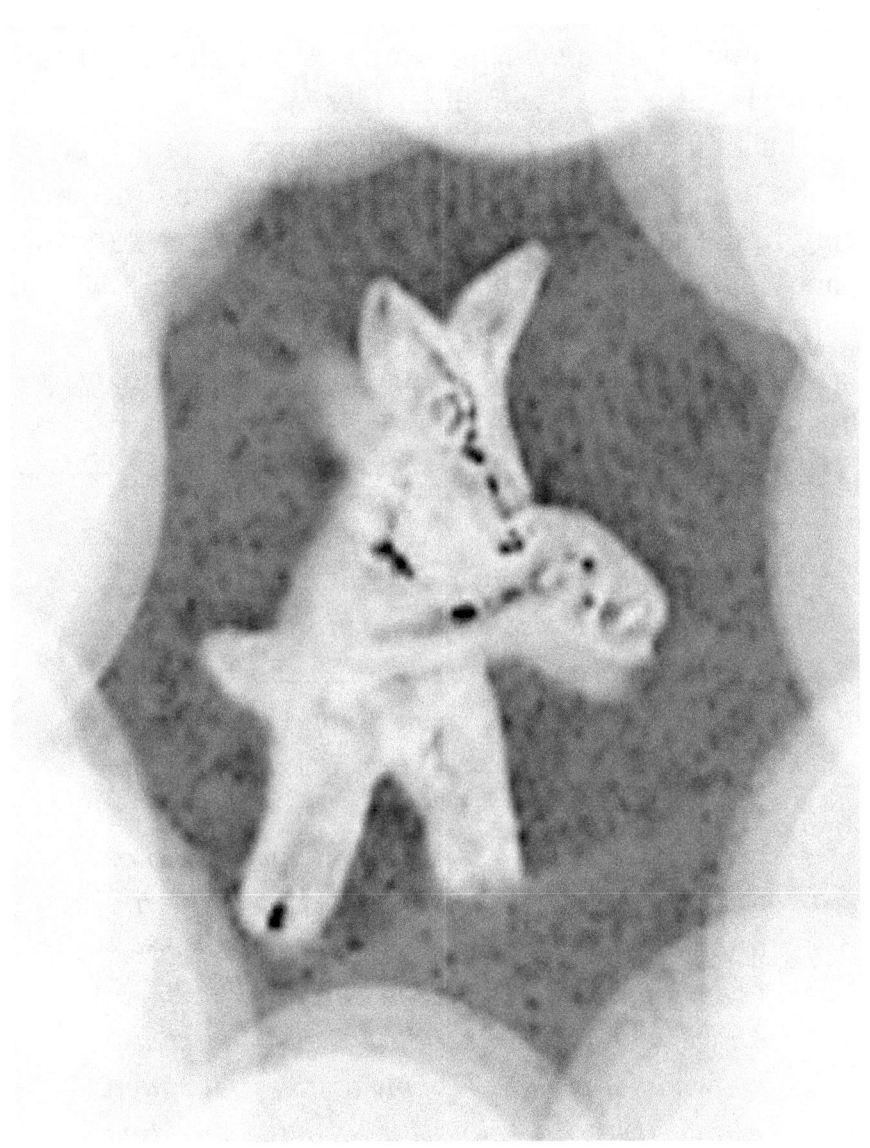

Instead, I pull out my phone and snap a picture or two. Modern technology is a wonderful thing in many ways, and I do not hesitate to make use of it for my own purposes, unlike some wise birds I can name, if I do not mind spending some time wearing cement overshoes and playing "I Spy With My Little Eye" with the fishies.

I shut the shelving unit and the pantry door and go sit in the front room. The discomfort generated by the small clay figure is so much less out here compared to in the pantry, it is bearable, although still not something I will go out of my way to experience.

I upload the picture to an image search app and, by and by, I find something.

> *The sun, according to the Andalupian islanders, is a wild dog, bright yellow in color. Each spring, she becomes pregnant by the moon, a wolf, and grows so large she fills the sky. When her water breaks, it drenches the barren earth and brings forth all living things. Her whelps are the stars. In her benign aspect, she nurtures and warms. In her savage aspect, she bites (sunburn, sunstroke, dehydration) or jealously guards her resources (causing drought, frost, freezes, hypothermia). Known under many names, depending on her aspect and effect (see link below), but generally known as Aa. As with many deities associated with fertility, Aa's rituals involve the shedding and consumption of blood. She is often depicted sucking the marrow from a human bone.*

Not a kazoo, after all.

So, where does the little yellow figure in the pantry come from? Who makes a secret shrine for her? Does a previous owner of the house have a housekeeper or houseboy from the island of Andalupia?

I wish Jasper Caufmann is still here, which is possibly the only time anybody ever wishes for such a thing. I wish to question him as follows: Does his routine with his finger, just before he kicks the shrine open, indicate a cut deep enough to bleed? If so, it is possible that his sticking his own bleeding finger into his mouth is interpreted by the goddess as a call to life.

Personally, I think that, if this is, indeed, the case, the goddess is stretching a point, but who am I to quibble with a goddess, especially one with the power of intense sunlight, if you get my drift?

Come to that, this is possibly why this particular goddess is looking for any excuse to activate: she is stuck in this hidden shrine for who knows how long, and suddenly the house is occupied by a guy who has her on the brain. True, what he wants to do is avoid her, but he is still obsessed, in his own way.

I make my plans and wait.

As the evening shadows begin to fall, the creepy feeling fades. The front door opens and Jasper Caufmann returns, which is not much of an improvement, at that.

"Well," he says, much astonished, "this is indeed a pleasant surprise. To what do I owe this charming visit?"

"I am here all day" I say. "Do you not remember?"

"I do not. If you are here all day, I am certain I do not leave." He smiles as if he thinks I will be happy to see it.

I hit him with another shot of glamour and his eyes become not just watery, but also blank.

"Come with me," I say.

"Yes, master," he intones.

Universal Studios has a lot to answer for, although they do not ask my opinion about it.

He follows me into the kitchen, where I take a paper towel and swab off his neck with half a flask of bourbon, which I carry in my pocketbook for just such emergencies. Then he follows me into the pantry.

I open the shrine. The feeling of threat is lower, now that night is coming on, but I am still queasy, or perhaps that is because of what I am about to do.

"Great Aa," I say, "accept this sacrifice and be once more at peace. Return to your little yellow statue and haunt this house no more." For good measure, I add, "I so plead with the magic words oogiddy boogiddy . . . please and thank you."

Then I move Jasper Caufmann's crucifix aside, bite him on the neck, and drink some of his blood.

It is not half bad, at that, although I have had better, to be sure.

As I swallow, I feel the remnants of the ominous atmosphere in the pantry recede and vanish.

That night, I am expecting Vlad the Roumanian to call, so I am not startled when the telephone rings and he asks if I have time for a little talk.

Naturally, anybody who enjoys wind in her hair rather than, say, six feet of dirt will always have plenty of time for idle chit-chat with Vlad the Roumanian.

I begin by making my report.

"This Magyar of Mr. Mansfield Parker's," I say, "does, indeed, abandon his post, but not without cause." I tell Vlad the Roumanian everything, not omitting my going so far as to bite Jasper Caufmann on the neck, which I, personally, think is worthy of many, many get out of jail free cards for me, indeed.

"All this," says Vlad the Roumanian, "is very interesting, indeed, but it is beside the point. Mr. Mansfield Parker is lonely in his Craftsman style bungalow, and decides to sell it and move into an assisted unliving facility, where he can be among others of his own kind."

"I hope he will be very happy," I say, as courtesy never goes out of style.

"There is just one thing."

I am afraid to ask if this one thing has anything to do with me, as it is almost a sure bet that it does or Vlad the Roumanian will not invest the wear and tear on his finger dialing my number.

"Mr. Mansfield Parker," Vlad the Roumanian says, "is, of course, a gentleman. He does not hire a guy to be his Magyar and then simply cast him aside when he no longer requires his services."

"He should eat in good health," I say, hopeful that this is where this particular conversation is going, although I know in my silent heart that it is not.

"Mr. Mansfield Parker," says Vlad the Roumanian, with the inevitability of Universal Studio's Wolf Man when the camera shows a shot of the full moon, "wishes me to find employment for his Magyar. Naturally," he says, "I think of you."

Personally, I wonder if I can shoot myself in the head with a silver bullet before the next sentence comes out, but

Pajr of Nosmal What?

I do not have a silver bullet. Even if I do, it will not do me much good, as I also do not have a gun.

Vlad the Roumanian continues as follows: "I tell Mr. Mansfield Parker that my good friend Miss Garnet Satin has a shop, and that she can certainly find various uses for a regular guy who is accustomed to working for Us. This, I tell him, will be most handy for you, satisfactory for the Magyar, and convenient for any of Us who may need the services of an investigative team such as the two of you make."

"We are not," I begin, but I clap my hand over my mouth before I can continue.

"You start to say something?" Vlad the Roumanian's voice does not need to sound dangerous, as his reputation takes care of details like that for him.

"We are not able to be any happier than this makes us," I say. "What a wonderful idea. I look forward to a long and happy investigative partnership."

After all, I tell myself, if things get too bad, I can always fetch the lead-lined box from the top shelf of my closet, open somebody's vein in front of the little yellow figure inside it, and see what happens.

Ghostly Conversations
by Dirk Grffin

i hear the dead
mumbling in every corner

they are waiting
one hand on my heart

blowing coldly in my ear

The Prince's Bride

by Ginny Fleming

The night of Saint Dunstan's Feast, Sarah stole secret glances across the great banquet table at her heart's desire. The King's younger son seemed as attractive inside as he was handsome. His shiny black hair hung in sensuous ringlets falling to strong shoulders and long dark lashes hooded his deep blue eyes. Just to gaze upon Prince Nikolai caused the girl's breath to catch in her throat and made her palms sweat.

She lost herself in a delicious fantasy bringing her fondest desire to life in her daydream. In her girlish imagination, she gazed into the prince's cobalt eyes, traced a quivering finger down his gorgeous face, begged his blessing to simply touch his strong chest and linger precious moments in ecstasy, feeling his heart beat. . . .

Suddenly, she caught Nikolai smiling in her direction and her heart soared even as her cheeks burned. But alas, the prince's smile was meant for the girl seated to her side and it was all Sarah could do to hold back her tears.

Sarah watched Nikolai flirt with the beautiful Laureli, whose golden hair caught the warm glow of the candles in the massive chandelier suspended over his father's bountiful table. It was rumored Laureli would never be confused with the wittier ladies of the Kingdom; but it mattered little. All of the eligible young men (and quite a few of the married ones) seemed in competition to coax a smile or a shy giggle from the comely maiden.

The fetching girl's green eyes sparkled much like the emeralds decorating her delicate yellow gown's low-cut bodice, causing Sarah to feel like a drab polk-weed overshadowed by a delicate flower. For although Cletus, Sarah's father, was a well-respected merchant in the Kingdom and known to be fiercely loyal to the King, it was his unspoken sorrow to sire a daughter as plain as she was skinny.

"Sarah?" Laureli lightly touched her arm in a whispered aside. "Is it true? Are you to be Bartlett's bride?"

Sarah looked into the emerald green eyes of the golden-haired beauty, "'Tis only rumor," she mumbled, "I've pledged to no man."

"Pity," Laureli said sweetly, "you'd make such a . . . lovely bride. And good Bartlett is indeed a prize. Why, any girl in the Kingdom would leap at the chance to be held in his strong arms."

Then, why don't I see you leaping? Sarah thought. But she remained silent. Her simple-minded friend wouldn't understand.

The night before, Sarah wept silently in the darkness of her bed. The recent death of wealthy swine-baron Bartlett's wife served to unnerve the plain girl. The unfortunate woman died birthing her last son and the noble swineman was looking to find a good wife and mother for his babe.

True, Bartlett was a comely man; his muscles strained provocatively under his rough work-shirt and a rawhide tie held his long blond hair secure. His fair features were nearly the contrasting equal to Prince Nikolai's dark beauty. But for all of Bartlett's comeliness, he still smelled of pig and silence was Sarah's answer to her father's question as he hefted the small bag of gold coins sent by Bartlett as a pledge for his daughter's hand.

Pair of Normal What?

Sarah spent her days learning the ways of the women of the village. She was accomplished in the kitchen, adept with a needle and thimble, could coax sweet music from a flute and it was said she'd make some man a good wife someday. Not a beautiful consort. Not an enchanting bride. But a good wife nevertheless.

She left the banquet table thinking of the handsome, though pungent, pig-farmer, telling herself her heart wasn't in a marriage where she'd only be a replacement for a dead woman . . . a warm spot in a cold bed — a cold bed ripe with the fragrance of pig. Besides, she wanted Prince Nikolai.

Taking her seat beside her father in the plush family carriage, Sarah smiled, the solution to her dilemma coming to mind, "Father?" she caressed his huge hand and batted her eyes coquettishly (an action which only magnified her plainness, had she but known), "Father? Grant me but one wish before I leave your house to wed good Bartlett?"

"Surely, Sarah," Cletus replied, pleased his child was settling to the notion of an honest life wed to a prosperous pig-farmer. True, the old man hoped for a better station in life for his only daughter. But plain she was and Cletus knew in his heart Bartlett's pledge would be Sarah's only offer. "Anything for my dear daughter."

"Might I have Bartlett's purse to purchase a fine trousseau from Andrew the tailor?" Sarah implored. "You realize, as the mistress of a swine-farm, I shan't have many fineries in my life."

Again she batted her eyes and Cletus felt the urge to tell Sarah how such flirtations brought out her plainness ten-fold. But, he held his tongue. He'd no wish to cause his daughter grief. She was surely plain, but she possessed a beautiful heart and he loved her nonetheless.

"What a grand idea!" old Cletus crowed. "Take this pouch of gold and buy the loveliest wedding gown Andrew can stitch! And at least five silk frocks besides! With matching slippers! Just because you are to be the bride of a pi . . . farmer doesn't mean you can't turn a fancy ankle at the King's celebrations."

"Look, Father!" Sarah cried, "We're nearly at Andrew's Shoppe! Pray, might I speak with him now?"

Cletus laughed and instructed his driver to pull to the front of the tiny establishment, "It makes my heart sing to see your exuberance! Bartlett will be a happy man, indeed!"

Sarah waved, watching her father's carriage continue toward their manor-house. She waited in the tailor's doorway until her father was out of sight, then crossed the dirty street taking care not to soil her party slippers. Approaching a coach for hire, she spoke sternly to the driver, "There's a gold coin for you if you'll deliver me to the door of the woman, Kurstain."

"You mean, the old witch-woman what lives at the foot of the mountain?" the common-born cabby snorted, "my lady, why would the likes of you desire. . . ."

"There's another gold coin if you do your job and hold your tongue in the bargain."

"Two gold coins?" the man snorted again, opened the door of his small rig and offered his hand to assist Sarah's entrance. "M'lady, I'd deliver the devil himself at Kurstain's door for two gold coins — and hold me tongue to boot!"

It was a rough ride to the small cottage nestled at the foot of the mountain. This common coach wasn't a luxury carriage like her father's and Sarah took the striking difference as a premonition of her future life with Bartlett. No matter this hired buggy lacked the stink of pig, she still felt the urgency to seek council with the witch-woman.

Pajr of Normal What?

Sarah instructed the cabby to wait beside the old woman's gate and she rapped three times on the cottage door. The old woman answering had a head full of long white hair as wild as a honeysuckle bush. She was withered and bent, but the strength of her voice belied her frailty.

"Girl, my powers are not for one such as you." the old woman stated this bluntly in exchange for greeting while closing the door in Sarah's face.

"Wait!" the girl stuck her foot in the doorjamb, "hear me out! A coin from this pouch of gold should buy me audience. And if after listening you refuse me, then keep the coin with my blessing. But, if indeed, you see fit to help — the whole purse is yours."

The old woman studied Sarah's face and judged her sincere, "Come in." She shook her head and opened the door, allowing Sarah to enter her modest cottage. "As you can clearly see I could put a coin or two to good use."

Kurstain indicated a three-legged chair at a roughhewn table and Sarah graciously took a seat.

"Now, Girl. Tell me what calamity brings you to my door."

Sarah sighed and spoke one word: "Love."

Kurstain snorted mockingly, "Of course, love. Love brings everyone to my door. Jealous love, selfish love, romantic love . . . love of power, love of money . . . love of evil. Love truly causes the Earth to spin. Which sort of love brings you to me?"

This time Sarah held her head high, "I must have Prince Nikolai."

"You don't ask for much, do you Girl?" Kurstain shook her head, laughing, "I've heard the prince is the handsomest man in the Kingdom — though I've never been fortunate enough to gaze upon his beauty and. . . ."

"If I don't have the prince, I will die!" Sarah interrupted the old woman.

"Nonsense, Girl!" Kurstain chuckled, "no woman has ever died for want of a man."

"It will be my death," the girl moaned, "and I'll die a pig-farmer's wife."

"So, you've come to beg me to witch the prince into falling in love with you?"

Sarah shook her head, "No . . . I realize any spell cast on the prince would be fleeting and false. I'm sure your brews and potions would bring me Prince Nikolai's kisses and affections for a time. . . . But, I want so much more. I want his soul."

"His soul?"

"I want to be his first vision at the dawn and his last dream at night," Sarah closed her eyes and raised her fingertips to her lips as if feeling the prince's kiss, "I hunger to hold him in my arms and gaze into the bottomless blue pools of his eyes. I crave the luxury to bury my hands in his black curls while he grants my every dream come true with his kisses. I need Nikolai to draw his very breath from me!"

"Romantic child."

The girl hissed, "I love Nikolai as a woman."

"Then I must ask you — and take care how you answer." The old woman took Sarah's chin in her gnarled hand. "Are you willing to sacrifice everything to win his soul?"

Sarah answered immediately, "Everything! Yes, and more!"

"There may be a way. . . ." the old woman mumbled. Hobbling to the dry sink by the far wall, she grabbed three herbs drying by the window and crushed them with a stone mortar and pestle. Kurstain then poured a foul liquid from a tiny pink flask on the flakes of herbs, wetting them into a sticky mush.

Looking over the old witch's shoulder, Sarah gagged in disgust, "You don't expect me to drink that, do you?"

"I should hope not," Kurstain snorted, "it would rot you from the inside out — not a pretty sight. Not a pretty sight at all!"

"Then, if it's not for drink, what is its usage?"

"So many pesky questions from one who desires such huge magic," the witch-woman grumbled. She reached over her head, removed a dusty book from a shelf, leafed through the yellowed tome and placed her claw-like finger in the middle of a page, "Here. Just where I remembered it."

"What are you going to. . . ."

"Questions!" Kurstain hushed the girl. "Now, hold your tongue while I speak the words. One slip of the spell and you could wind up with donkey ears . . . or worse!"

Sarah forced herself to silence, watching the old witch read the magical instructions. "The bones of one who died for love," Kurstain clapped her hands together, reached into a blue jar filled to the brim with a gray lumpy powder and took a generous pinch between her fingers.

"Remains of a gallant knight. . . ." the old woman chuckled, "Died trying to save me from that angry demon I conjured. But, that was years ago — and another story altogether. Next ingredient, let's see. . . . Bones of one who died for beauty. Well, Lover," she gazed fondly at the jar of gray dust, "it appears it's you again," turning to Sarah, Kurstain giggled and dipped into the dried knight once more, "I was a beauty in my day," the old witch-woman looked to Sarah as if waiting for the girl to refute her claim. "Back to the book. Bones of one who died for glory. Hhumm. That's a tough one. Tristan fought for many things, but glory was not one of his battles. Let's see what . . . I mean, who I have stored in the cupboard."

The old woman opened the tall wooded cabinet and searched for many minutes among the jars and bottles secreted in the dark corners of the sideboard, "Ah-ha! I'd forgotten you were hiding in there, George!"

Kurstain held the purple jar high, "George fought dragons. Had an obsession with the scaly green demons. Myself, I avoid dragons. I find them boring and trite. But, I suppose," she said, pulling the cork from the jar's mouth and taking a pinch of George, "dying in the attempt to save a king's daughter from a huge fire-breathing lizard could be considered a glorious means to an end. So!" she cackled, dropping the last item of the incantation into the small stone dish, "now we have the proof of love, beauty and glory."

She snapped her fingers three times over the sticky concoction causing a green puff of smoke to erupt from the little bowl. The old witch cautiously looked into the mortar, noticing the wet herbs and lumpy dust now appeared to be a pile of dried spice. She cackled again, "*This* will be the magic potion in your quest of Prince Nikolai's soul."

"Magic potion?" Sarah murmured, "But, you said it wasn't to drink."

"Smart girl!" Kurstain snorted, "You don't drink it. You don't chew it. You don't rub it on your skin."

Sarah reached out a hesitant finger and waited for the witch's silent permission to touch the cinnamon-like powder. "It must be very powerful. . . ."

152

"In the right hands, enough of this powder could change the course of history," the old woman whispered in reverence. She cleared her throat, shook her head and continued. "Tell me. Has Prince Nikolai shown interest in another?"

"Laureli, the high-sheriff's daughter."

The old woman eagerly nodded her head, "And is she pretty?"

Sarah smiled sadly, "Not just pretty. . . . She's beautiful. When she's in the room, Prince Nikolai takes notice of no other."

"Good!" Kurstain crowed.

The girl stood, angry and ready to leave. She snatched Bartlett's purse from the table, "You crazy old. . . ."

"Wait!" the old witch-woman chuckled, "I meant — Good. She will aid your claim to the prince's soul. One word of caution. After the magic, you and the high-sheriff's daughter will be unable to speak of the spell. You are bound by the magic as it is bound by you," Kurstain chuckled again. "Sit down, Girl. Sit down and I will give you instruction to make your magic work."

Deep in thought, Sarah left the old witch-woman's cottage. The cabby opened the door on the small buggy and the girl presented him with two coins of the three she'd taken from Bartlett's purse before dropping it in Kurstain's outstretched hand. She held up the third and last coin and spoke quietly to the driver, "Sirrah, luck is with you tonight if you see me to the high-sheriff's door. Wait for me there — and then, no matter how much I protest — deliver me home to my father."

Pair of Normal What?

The door was answered by the high-sheriff's smiling housekeeper. Being unattractive herself she recognized a younger sister in plainness.

"Good evening, Teresa." Sarah returned the woman's sisterly smile. "Might I speak with Laureli?"

"Surely, Miss." Teresa showed the girl through to the sitting room. "My Laureli was only now preparing for sleep. I will announce you. Please have a seat, M'lady."

Moments later, Sarah looked up to see Laureli running delicately down the winding steps from her bedroom, "Sarah — Oh, Sarah! I'm so glad to see you! I must tell you my news!"

"News?"

Laureli skipped to Sarah's side and grabbed the other girl's hands in excitement, "Prince Nikolai!! Tonight, after the banquet, he begged me linger as the guests were leaving. He pulled me out to the balcony, slipped this silver ring on my finger and kissed me. The Prince asked me to be his bride! Oh, Sarah — I'm going to be Princess Laureli!"

"I'm so happy for you. . . ." Sarah murmured.

"Just think of it," Laureli bubbled, oblivious to Sarah's pain, "we'll be brides together. You'll wed Bartlett and I'll be the Prince's bride. Won't we have such a merry time?"

Sarah forced herself not to grind her teeth, "Laureli, my dear friend. I've something for you."

"A present? A wedding present?"

"You might call it that," the girl grinned, "I purchased it tonight, just for you."

Laureli smiled and dimples erupted on her flawless face, "Dearest Sarah. How in Heaven's name did you know Nikolai would propose tonight? Are you a prophetess? No matter! How very like you to think of me on my day of betrothment, when you, yourself, are soon to become Bartlett's good wife."

Sarah grimaced, ground her teeth and opened the handkerchief holding the cinnamon-like powder, "I would die before allowing a pig-farmer to bed me." She blew the reddish dust into Laureli's surprised face and spoke Kurstain's words of magic: "Beauty, I claim thee as my own."

The room spun, Sarah closed her eyes and reached out to grab something, anything to regain her equilibrium. She could hear Laureli moaning as if the other girl were caught in the same swirling turbulence. The noise in her ears reached a deafening crescendo and Sarah cried out in pain.

When at last she could open her eyes, Sarah found herself grasping the arms of a girl wearing modest clothes, a plain girl dressed in a beige gown.

Still gripping the other girl's arms, she looked down at her own lap and recognized the yellow silk gown inlaid with emeralds so becoming on Laureli at the King's table.

"It worked!" Sarah whispered in Laureli's voice.

"What?" the plain girl murmured.

"I'm . . . beautiful!" Sarah ran her hands over her new body, ignoring the confused girl sitting before her wearing her old face.

"What?" the plain girl murmured again.

Sarah laughed, relishing the lilting giggles coming from her newly slender throat, "Really . . . Sarah," she addressed the other girl, "the night grows late and you must be going. By now, your father is surely frantic with worry."

"What?" Laureli cried, her new voice sounding harsh and guttural.

Sarah pushed the unfortunate plain girl from the house and into the arms of the carriage driver. She giggled again, closed the door, leaned against it and gazed into the foyer's full-length mirror, "Not only am I the most beautiful girl in the Kingdom, but I'm soon to be the Prince's bride. My new beauty will surely bring me true happiness!"

"Laureli's" wedding day came within weeks. The excitement and festivities were heady and delicious for the girl with the beautiful face. She filled her days with fittings and pampering, while saving her nights for chaperoned audiences with her future husband.

Their wedding day dawned bright and clear, the trumpeters heralded the royal couple as they performed the traditional march to the chapel and the people cheered Prince Nikolai walking hand in hand with his beautiful bride-to-be. The procession entered the chapel arbor and Prince Nikolai turned to Sarah whispering, "Your radiance outshines the sun. I'm the envy of every man in the Kingdom. See how they drink in your beauty? See how they. . . ."

Suddenly, the prince's deep voice was silenced. A heavy limb broke away from the overhead branches of a fragrant cherry tree striking the dark-haired handsome man square on the top of the head and he fell senseless to the ground. Sarah screamed, pulled Nikolai's beautiful head into her lap and watched his blood stain the front of her pearl-beaded wedding gown.

The prince awoke in his bed with Sarah pacing the floor while the finest medical men in the region hovered nearby. "Laureli?" he said, his voice sounded weak and pained, "Laureli? Where are you? Someone light the candles. . . ."

Sarah rushed to his side, "Nikolai, I am here. Don't struggle, my love. The doctors say you should be still and. . . ."

"Laureli!" Nikolai interrupted her, "summon Maggie. Have her fetch the lamps. Tell her I need candles. How do they expect me to see your beautiful face in this infernal darkness?"

The doctors pushed Sarah from the room and closed the door to her protests. Within minutes, the prince's door flew open and frantic people ran in all directions. Prince Nikolai was blind.

In the following hours, the medical men diagnosed Prince Nikolai's malady as pressure on the brain and prescribed the most modern treatment, but the leeches proved ineffective in their curative powers. By night's end, it was determined the prince would be blind for the rest of his life.

The very next morning, a young boy summoned Sarah to Prince Nikolai's side and she dried her tears, determined not to allow her soul-mate to know her sorrow. His blindness broke her heart, but she knew he'd have none of her pity. Sitting on the bed beside her heart's desire, she gazed into his blinded eyes and found them clear and to all appearances uninjured. Anyone meeting the prince would be unaware of his sightlessness. Sarah smiled, thankful for small favors. At least her prince's beautiful face was unmarred.

"Laureli?" Prince Nikolai asked, his hands searching the air around him, "Laureli? Is that you?"

It was a few moments before Sarah recognized her new name, "Yes, Nikolai. Yes, I'm here by your side."

Pair of Normal What?

"I'm so glad you came," the prince said, "I've fretted awake all night, wrestling with this horrible dilemma. . . ."

"Darling, put it out of your mind," Sarah cooed. "Blindness can not wrest my affections from you. I shall love you forever."

The prince shook his beautiful black mane and groped for Sarah's hand, "No, Laureli. No, you don't understand. I'm not wondering if you can still love me — I'm searching for the words to say I can't marry you."

Sarah was stunned. What were these strange utterances coming from Prince Nikolai's perfect lips? She laughed uneasily, "Nikolai . . . I told you your blindness matters not. I shall be your eyes, my love shall be your guide and. . . ."

"No, Laureli," Nikolai interrupted the girl again. "Listen carefully to my words. Because of my blindness and your beauty, I can't marry you. When I thought back on the moments before my accident, I remembered the men enjoying your loveliness. I remembered my words. . . . Drinking in your beauty. Then I was felled by the hand of fate. How can I go through life never to see your beautiful face? How can I stand the knowledge other men are savoring my wife's beauty when I cannot? Your beauty deserves sighted eyes. Go, marry a whole man. I set you free, Laureli."

"Nikolai, no!! You cannot do this!" Sarah protested, "you cannot set me free when I'm unwilling to leave!"

Nikolai shook his head sadly, not wishing to hurt the lovely Laureli any more than necessary, "I am the youngest son of the King," he gently said, "and I can. I've already had your name stricken from the banns and I've spoken with my father about arranging a marriage with old Cletus' daughter, Sarah."

Sarah stiffened. Tears fell freely, wetting her cheeks. She murmured, "But, Nikolai — Sarah is so plain . . . and . . . and she is betrothed to Bartlett the pig-farmer."

"As prince I have right to buy back Bartlett's purse and pledge," Prince Nikolai explained. "As far as Sarah's plainness, the better yet to be the wife of a blind man. Don't you see? By taking Sarah into my bed I shall not have to wonder if any other men are drinking in her beauty."

Sarah opened her lovely mouth to tell her beautiful dark-haired blue-eyed heart's desire she was indeed Cletus' plain daughter, but to her horror and dismay found she could not. The words would not leave her lips.

"Nikolai, I am Sar. . . . Please understand, Nikolai. I'm Sar. . . ." Try as she might, the words were not hers to give and for a moment she felt a pang of guilt for the other girl's most certain fruitless efforts attempting to explain away a horrible and sudden plainness.

Sarah recalled Kurstain's warning of spelled silence and she sighed, realizing the magic held her tongue as surely as she was now held prisoner to her new beauty. She silently shook her head, knowing how much truth was in the old saying: Beauty is in the eye of the beholder. For the prince, beauty was now a delicacy he denied himself. Although Sarah wanted to hate Prince Nikolai for his shallowness, she looked into her own heart so ruled by vanity and bitterly realized her prejudices.

"I wish you and La . . . Sarah a happy life. Nikolai," Sarah whispered, feeling her heart break, "might I have a last kiss?"

He nodded. Sarah leaned in, pressed her full lips to his perfect mouth, closed her eyes and wept for the life that would never be hers. And as she tasted the heady wine of Prince Nikolai's lips, she wondered how difficult it would prove to acclimate herself to the smell of pig.

This Ain't Normal, is it?

by Joanna Foreman

Back when I put this abandoned Amtrak passenger car on the rusty train tracks running parallel to Main Street, I thought I would be set for life. The Roswell Tooter — it's cramped in here, but I got a good thing goin' from my years as a cook in the U. S. Army. A grueling job, but it taught me a few things, so here I am, standin' at the grill. Tasty grub and the one-of-a-kind atmosphere draw a crowd at breakfast, lunch and dinner. But, this slump in the economy has led me to one conclusion: I gotta fire my sister's kid. Black hair, black eyeliner, black disposition. He's fried his brain with who knows what. Nothing normal about that boy. The way his lobes are plugged, they stretch into a zero shape, like his personality, and with the silver hoops hangin' from his eyebrows and bottom lip, he could be receivin' signals from outer space for all I know. Problem is, he ain't takin' his signals from *me*, the Chief Engineer. Good service — a major ingredient in my recipe for success — just ain't the boy's specialty. He's got to go. I hired him because of my sister. She can nag a man to death. So when my other waiter disappeared into thin air one day, (no call-no show — never even asked for his final paycheck) I didn't have much of a choice. Come to think of it, that other kid had just as much ink on his arms as the nephew. They must've used the same tattoo artist 'cause one arm has what they call a "sleeve" of nothin' but black lizards and one fine dragon with a snake wrapped around its gut from top to bottom; dark stuff. Kids these days.

Pair of Normal What?

The nephew's not my only worry, either. I'm losing customers faster than I can collect 'em. It looks to me like I might suffer three more casualties today if I don't do something fast.

The businessman comes in every morning with a briefcase and the daily news, wearing a white, long-sleeved shirt that looks like it just came off the ironing board. He's been a regular now for nearly six months — always slides into the same booth, the one nobody else wants because of the way the sun hits the window. There's an annoying glare that won't go away, even on cloudy days, and that ain't normal is it? Oh well. He orders Eggs Benedict, which really pisses me off 'cause that's extra work for me. Hollandaise sauce and poached eggs — I figure him for some kind of sissy-man. He drums on his fancy laptop computer while he fawns over the nephew's arm "sleeves" from his wrist to his biceps, but then he leaves a generous tip so the nephew never complains. The trouble? My other customers are waving their hands in the air for service and it's left to me to do reconnaissance. I nearly burnt a patty melt doing two jobs at once, just last week.

Right around lunch time, the college student with the brown ponytail rolls through the door on inline skates. She sits in the same booth as the man did, orders a small salad with low-fat dressing and a diet soda, opens her electronic notebook and goes through the same routine. Like a lover, she strokes the nephew's arms over and over, tracing her finger along the prickly dragon's tail like she's studying a map. Hell, it could be a map of some kind, for all I know. That boy's tattoos put me in the mind of a psychedelic art museum. You can stay all day and still not see everything and you gotta be on one substance or another to make sense of any of it. I'll admit, though, the dragon tail is a fine piece of work.

"You two got something goin' on over there?" I asked him once.

"Nah. Not really." Then, he winked. That boy — he's a piece of work, too.

Now the woman, well, she's another story altogether. Her short skirts and low-cut sweaters leave little to my imagination. Struts around on four-inch heels. She's fine. Right before she's due to come in at dinner time (after a long day at the office, I imagine), I turn the grill over to the nephew. I wash up and shave in the restroom. Splash of Old Spice. I can clean up nice if I want. And I want — I don't let nobody take this lady's order but me — the Chief Engineer.

"What'll it be today, young lady?" I always say that; it makes her smile.

She orders something different every day. To the extent of the menu, of course. Yesterday it was *chicken fried steak* and the day before that *chicken and dumplings,* and just last week she said she'd been craving *chicken fingers.* The lady does love her some chicken, all right. Chicken and her cell phone. She's poking around on her smart phone through the entire meal. I don't see how she manages with her fake nails.

"This your favorite booth?" I ask.

"What? Oh, yes. I get a particularly strong signal here," she says. I want to say, "I've got your signal right here, Chicken Lover," but I think better of it. She likely prefers a dignified type of man.

I place a plate in front of her. "I'm Harold, the Chief Engineer. Just holler if you need anything." Once, I was about to ask her out, but her cell phone rang and she turned away from me to answer it. I can take a hint. So I go back to the grill and relieve the nephew for his "smoke" break. I tell him he'd darn well better be hiding behind the dumpster with his roach, out of the keen eyesight of the silver badge in this dusty old town of Roswell.

Today, the businessman comes in as usual. Yeah, yeah, Eggs Benedict, I know. Everything's chill — people chatter, skillets sizzle, silverware clinks. But when the lady blows in on her way to work, that's when it's déjà vu for me. She ain't due in here till dinnertime.

The busboy found the lady's cell phone wedged between the seat and back of the booth last night. He put it up by the cash register in our Lost and Found basket. I'd hoped it wouldn't lead to this, but when she comes in early, I know I'm in trouble. She struts right over to the businessman before I can stop her.

"Did you, by chance, find a little pink cell phone on the seat?"

He glances up from his paper. "No. I'm sorry. Are you sure it was in this booth?"

"Absolutely. I never sit anywhere else." She clicks her heels across the floor to the cash register where I'm standin' with her pink electronic gadget in my hand. My eyes are on the man; his are on the woman.

"Oh, thank you," she gushes as she retrieves her phone. "I owe you one."

"No problem. See you at dinnertime." She looks put-out, disappointed that I'm not all flirty, like usual. Well, ordinarily I'd try to get a conversation goin', ask her out, but not today. I've got a catastrophe to prevent and I want her out of my diner! She harrumphs and heads toward the exit, clicking those red heels and swiveling her curvy rear-end.

"I see you've found your device," says the man in the booth as the lady passes by.

She stops cold.

The top of my head sweats underneath my conductor's cap. Not again, I tell myself. Oh God, please not again. Good customers are too hard to come by.

At that, the lady sits herself down across from the man and they're whispering, all hush-hush. I'll have to usher them out before college gal comes if I'm gonna dodge the bullet. I motion to the nephew.

"Get 'em both outta here." I nod my head toward the booth. "Tell him you wanna collect from him 'cause you're goin' on break." The nephew looks at me like I've gone mad. "Now!"

"Okay, Dude, take it easy." He rips the green check off its pad and hands it to the man, talking so low I can't hear.

He saunters back, a sour look on his puss, the check in his hand with a twenty-spot. "Dude says he's not ready to leave just yet, so 'take the money, kid, and leave us alone.' What a skank. I'm gonna teach him a lesson."

I hold the boy back. "No. You just need to disappear for now. I'll handle this." I send him outside with the busboy for another smoke break. I head for the door to lock it. Too late. Ponytail girl skates in with her eyes half shut, buds in her ears, and rolls into the booth. She squeals, jolted to find herself inadvertently in the lap of the businessman, although I'd lay odds the man was more than pleased. I'm showing her to another table, but the other two won't hear anything of it. "Join us," they say.

Pajr of Nomal What?

It's the weirdest thing. Just like last fall. Same thing happened only with different customers.

Back at the cash register now, I can't do nothin' but watch. And shake my head. The three of them finally go out the front door together and make their way back behind the train. I know that's the last I'll see of *that* set of regulars. Déjà vu, like I said before.

A gasping busboy runs in and drags me to the rear window to watch another episode of my abnormal life, already in progress. Out by the dumpster, four human silhouettes dissolve in static, little by little. A heap of tattoos lie on the ground, like a yellowed set of maps from days gone by. A gust of wind from nowhere blows them into oblivion like ashes from an old campfire. I remove my conductor cap and scratch my head. So *that's* the way it is. Guess I won't have to sack the nephew after all.

Scarecrows

by Janet Wolanin Alexander

As the bus snaked down the mountain road
I saw downhill to my left,
on a precious piece of flatland,
a field scattered with survivors from the fall harvest.
Standing in the crop stubble
were not one, not two, but four scarecrows!
What were the sentries discussing at their convention—
switching watch posts or acquiring new spring wardrobes?

Alpha

by J. Baumgartle

It was with her still after all these years, though in a lesser degree, the quality she had since dubbed Alpha. Friends and neighbors recognized it in her and didn't know what to make of it, afraid to get too close for fear it would rub off. Its intensity constantly outlined a person with an almost visible, certainly perceptible aura of energy. Everyone in her family had it when she was a kid. The family dentist remarked on it: "You people are always on the edge." She laughed, at the moment poised by the table with a hummingbird's still-motion, sipping tea.

Diana supposed that was as good a description as any. It wasn't nerves, or random jitters, more like a hyper-sensitivity that extended to all areas of your life. Whatever it was, it had been there from the beginning and made the family, for better or worse, set apart.

Other people, she'd discovered, lived their lives speaking from chairs, or standing, discussing whatever was of interest to them. —Talking furniture, they seemed, placed like toy figures on a street corner or in a doll house, in an attitude of living. You wanted to move them, drape towels over their arms, march them up and down steps, use the tips of their plastic fingers to push open doors.

This fault she perceived in the outside world had been accentuated by the mental lethargy she'd met in school. The teacher's lesson was spelled out ad infinitum as Diana waited, pencil poised, ready for the word Go. Bang! The imaginary gun went off and she was scribbling for all she was worth, both hands on the paper, smudging the leaded lines as she wrote. Pencil smashed down; the paper was deposited like a secret document on the teacher's desk. —Afterglow.

The warmth dissipating; twiddling the pencil between fingers; biting nails. Would they never finish? Studying the material of her dress. The gathers, caught at the waistline, swelled from little hills and valleys to a rolling fabric meadow across her legs. Also aware of the feet one had to keep to oneself, of the grain of the wood floor changing abruptly where one piece butted up against another, a puzzle that became familiar in time. A suppressed yawn.

Eventually somebody else took her paper up, followed by another and another. The rest would float in like unhurried autumn leaves, always one clinging to the tree long after the others had fallen, and having to stay in at recess. Passing eternity in the privacy of her own thoughts, becoming so deeply involved in them that it startled her when the bell rang—

All her life had been like that, she thought, a process of hurry-up, wait. What good was it to gaze through the leaping flames of your soul? It only made you dissatisfied with what you saw.

She placed the earthenware mug on the red place-mat. Red: a color most people enjoyed. She found it garish and only used the mats because they were a gift from her mother-in-law, who would be coming to dinner.

Tonight they would all sit in the living room till time to eat, then sit in the dining room, then sit in the living room again when dinner was over. She didn't remember anyone in her immediate family ever sitting down, except to meals, and then no one quite touched the seat of his chair. They all talked at once, eating like crazy (though none of them ever gained a pound), trifles of daily pathos intermingling with Dad's jokes; Mom, knowing we were all out of hand, deciding not to care. The minute the last bite of dessert was downed, they split to the four winds and the house again became a beehive of activity.

We were comfortable with each other, she thought, in a way that we children have never been since we left home, due to that unique behavior. Alpha was like being possessed. Whatever your will or intentions, you had to obey it, give way to your feelings, become a hero or a villain, act on impulse.

For that reason, they all seemed to have sought oblivion, to protect themselves and those their lives touched. Her parents had found it on a wooded hillside, geographically isolated from neighbors, work, church, school. As adults her brothers and sisters had each sought a soul-mate, and been content to find approval there.

To "fit in" or not never bothered them; they weren't raised to it. Their parents were as different as night and day, conflict an accepted fact of life. Yet the family unit held; all were loved. Perhaps they thrived on that diversity. In fact, when things got boring, they'd stir up a little controversy just to have something to explore — some far reaching, soul-searching, even unnerving foray into philosophical questions — content to hug each other goodnight at a given hour, happily lost.

Ah, how she missed that. College had been a reprieve of sorts — a couple of teachers, friends, her first love, had all been similarly afflicted–but out here, in the "real" world, thinking was not considered a recreation, just something done grudgingly when it couldn't be avoided. Tonight, she knew what to expect at dinner, and was prepared to paint eyeballs on her eyelids.

Yet this was the way of life she had chosen. She had purposefully married outside of Alpha, wanting a life in the only world that existed. Darned if she'd condemn her children to being hermits! But it was hard to negate her own influence. Most times her daughter and son appeared normal, but under the light of in-law's scrutiny, you could see they were both tainted. Hooray! I failed, she would think, and then sigh for them as they struggled under their handicap.

Alpha. It was the most compelling force in her life and accounted for everything from her religious fervor to the bizarre (according to some) way she dressed. She'd tried to subjugate it in every way possible — it had seemed important at one time to be in control of one's life — but it always emerged stronger than ever, shredding complacency, demanding sacrifice. Why does it manifest itself in self-destructive tendencies, she wondered? It is talent laced with eccentricity, love that stretches its arms to include lepers, discovery that won't be denied; heaven help me, the sublime to the ridiculous.

Finally, at the age of forty-four, she had decided to come to terms with it, take the advantages it gave her, move past the separation it caused and be content. She was always going to speak her mind and rock boats, but she could at the same time care immensely about those who were in them. Age had its advantages. With maturity, people supposed you to be more solid emotionally, less off-the-wall. —Not that "matronly" was anything she wanted to become. Why should gray hair terminate her feminine identity. She intended to be well-kept, soft and sweet under ninety years of wrinkles, and not lose her sense of humor. Great music was not to be apologized for anymore, but played at the beach if she felt like it—

Control; control was an illusion, as was life, an experience borrowed out of time, and time passed so quickly. She thought of her father, alone now on the hill. In a frenzy of performance all his life, his Alpha was dimming, becoming little more than a light behind his eyes. In time the flame burned down, she knew. Even a year ago she'd been able to physically lift her teen-aged daughter — mid protests — but now something warned her not to. Tendons would snap, her spine would crumble — not worth the risk. Her juggling would have to take a different form now. The two of them would balance wits, compare men, study clothes . . . .

The incredible aspirations she saw in her daughter made her want to throw water on them — big ventures were not unassociated with big losses (she'd known her share), but could you really do that? Alpha was strong; it thrived on resistance—

Hmmm. A slow smile crept across her face — a little resistance. . . .

Written before the described condition had a name: Attention Deficit Hyperactivity Disorder: ADHD.

Contributors

The Southern Indiana Writers Group has been more-or-less together since 1992. We began meeting monthly in a conference room in a local hospital. We now meet weekly to exchange information and expertise on everything from computers to poetry. The group also serves as a critique forum (in the same sense that a pack of wolves serves as food critics). Membership is limited, but visitors are welcome, and have been known to fit in so well they become members against their better judgment.

Bonnie Abraham After twenty-five plus years of writing letters disqualifying people from Unemployment Benefits, she retired in order to write something more pleasant. She writes short stories (many with Biblical themes), poetry and devotionals. Currently, she resides in Corydon with her mother's ghost.

Jan Wolanin Alexander retired science teacher married to a biology professor, mother of 10 fur-children: 1 horse, 4 dogs, and 5 cats, custom horsehair jewelry maker, part-time dog kennel worker, writer of horse tales, trail rider.

Marian Allen lives in a big house in a little wood, which is not the only difference between Allen and Laura Ingels Wilder. She has published stories in print and on-line magazines, including Marion Zimmer Bradley's FANTASY Magazine, The Phone Book, PanGaia and Oceans of the Mind. She blogs at marianallen.com.

Pair of Normal What?

Jeannine Baumgartle writes poetry and fiction. Her work has appeared in publications such as *Green Meadow Press, Flying Island, Literally*, and Studio: *A Journal for Christians Writing* and won a residency for poetry at the Mary Anderson Center for the Arts . She and her husband live in the small town of Crandall.

Ginny Fleming considers herself to be foremost a screenwriter, as this is her favorite media. Because nobody thought to tell her she couldn't, after optioning 3 scripts for the unsold ensemble sitcom *"Tia"* (any producers reading this?), Fleming dived head-first into the shark-infested mulligan stew (How's that for mixing metaphors?) that is Hollywood scriptwriting. Fleming's take on hysterical fantasy (funny, that is), a novel she likes to call *Dragonsayver* (when she's not calling it Marvin), is a "Shrek-like" novel just begging to be made into an animated film (Fleming wonders if she should shove a tin cup in its hand and drop it on a busy intersection). Besides her annual contribution to SIW anthology and a brief appearance in the Louisville Courier-Journal, Fleming is busy finding a home for *Keys of Illusion*, a Romantic/Suspense novel filled with magic, scuba, fantasy, a bunch of lavender stuff and little bit of sex. Multiple scripts are always in the works whenever Fleming manages to "channel" Jimmy Buffett, her "Muse" (Yeah, she knows Jimmy's not dead — Hopes for his continued good health, in fact — That just makes him easier to channel).

Joanna Foreman's memoir *The Know-It-All Girl* was published in January, 2013 by Hydra Publishing. Her short fiction has appeared in The Indian Creek Anthology Series; Melange-Books; and a self-published collection of ghost stories titled *Ghostly Hauntings of Interstate-65*. She enjoys experimenting with health-conscious recipes for dinner, then ruins it all with decadent delicacies for dessert. Her éclairs and pastries were a hit at Stella's Café in New Albany, Indiana during the mid-1990s. She will do laundry and ironing as necessary, but has never acquired a taste for housecleaning and has no intention of doing so anytime soon. She grew up in Indianapolis, raised her three sons in Louisville and currently resides in Georgetown, IN. If wishes came true, Joanna would spend summer months in St. Augustine at the beach with her grandchildren. She blogs nostalgia at www.joannaforeman.wordpress.com Visit her website at www.joannaforeman.com.

Dirk Griffin, also known as The Invisible Man. Dirk is seldom among us in reality, but reality has never been our strong suit, anyway. He has written theatre reviews for Arts Kentuckiana, had a script produced for Public Access Television, and has written music/lyrics and/or scripts for several musicals. Bunbury Theatre of Louisville, Kentucky, selected one of Griffin's plays, *Plastic Jesus*, to include in their 2001 15th Anniversary 15 Minute Play Festival.

T Lee Harris is a scribbler of the lowest order. Not only does she pen lies about people who don't exist, but she draws pictures of them as well. Harris has also been known to aid and abet others by putting their scribblings into book form and even going so far as to devise covers for these publications. She claims she went to school to learn these things, but that shouldn't be held against anyone.

Harris is, in turn, aided and abetted by others in her assaults against literature. Among these accomplices are Hydra Publications, who have shamelessly published her untruths about an ancient Egyptian scribe and a magic temple cat; Untreed Reads, who have promulgated her lies about a retired spy who keeps getting mixed up in other people's business, and the Southern Indiana Writers' Group — possibly the worst offenders of all — who have permitted her to commit her acts of literary vandalism with their Indian Creek Anthology Series, not once, but at total of 18 times to date.

There are suspicions that Harris is committing a novel or two, but this has yet to be confirmed.

Samantha Lopez grew up in Houston, Texas. She graduated from Southern Illinois University at Carbondale in Illinois, moved to Chicago, and is now in the Louisville area. When not fighting her two cats for the computer, she browses bookstores, practices various musical instruments, volunteers at sci-fi conventions, and attends Renaissance festivals. She writes science fiction, fantasy, mainstream, and poetry. Her poetry has been published in Nightlife newspaper. She is currently working on several novels.

Glenda Mills resides in New Albany, Indiana with her husband and youngest son. She has a daughter and a son who no longer live at home and two grandchildren. When she is not busy homemaking, homeschooling, attending soccer games, running the family taxi service, or volunteering at her church, she writes fiction, nonfiction, and poetry. She looks forward to the day when a person can actually be in two places at once.

www.ingramcontent.com/pod-product-compliance
Lightning Source LLC
Chambersburg PA
CBHW071212260626
47162CB00004B/1265